SLEEPING IN THE BLOOD

Robert Richardson was born in Manchester in 1940. Since 1960 he has been a journalist, working for many years on the *Daily Mail* and contributing to, among others, the *Independent*, the *Guardian* and the *Sunday Times*. He is married with two sons and lives in Old Hatfield. Robert Richardson is also the author of *The Latimer Mercy*, *Bellringer Street*, *The Book of the Dead*, *The Dying of the Light* and *The Lazarus Tree*; all of which are published by Gollancz.

Also by Robert Richardson in Gollancz Crime

THE LATIMER MERCY
BELLRINGER STREET
THE BOOK OF THE DEAD
THE DYING OF THE LIGHT

SLEEPING IN THE BLOOD

by

Robert Richardson

GOLLANCZ CRIME

Gollancz Crime is an imprint of Victor Gollancz Ltd
14 Henrietta Street, London WC2E 8QJ

First published in Great Britain 1991
by Victor Gollancz Ltd

First Gollancz Crime edition 1992

A catalogue record for this book
is available from the British Library

ISBN 0-575-05319-4

Printed and bound in Great Britain
by Cox & Wyman Ltd, Reading

Author's Note

For those interested in such curiosities, the tomb of Dame Mary Page with its strange inscription referred to on pages 22 and 23 can be found in Bunhill Fields graveyard on the City Road in London, next to which are the offices of *The Independent*, the original of *The Chronicle*. However, while Dame Mary really existed, any journalists in this book do not—or at least only their names have been borrowed.

Prologue: June, 1968

Like a silent film in slow motion, Barry Kershaw somersaulted through humid Maida Vale night air from the penthouse balcony of the block of flats, until by some chance of distance his forehead crashed on to the concrete slabs of the courtyard and his skull split open. Crouched in a moon-shadowed bush, a hunting cat jumped away with a squeal of fright as the echo of the impact smacked round the walls, then there was stillness again. From the balcony, silhouetted against the lighted room behind her, a girl looked down at the body, Bob Dylan's 'Tambourine Man' floating out into the sticky darkness. She waited, then, when nobody appeared, went back inside, closing the french doors. Tapering heels of knee-length black leather boots leaving indentations in the Persian carpet, she crossed to one of the tables covered in bottles and the remains of food, poured a Bacardi and Coke then sat on the couch, mini-skirted legs visible far up her thighs.

She stared at a signed poster of Herman and the Hermits on the wall as the album finished and there were a series of clicks from the record-player as the automatic mechanism dropped another album into place. The sound of the Beach Boys filled the room as the girl smoked thoughtfully. Mentally she counted the names of those she knew had been in the flat during the evening. There were nineteen, plus about another dozen who had been strangers. It had not been a party, just a collection of visitors calling in *en route* to some West End theatre or Soho nightclub. Barry had only needed to make a few phone calls to let it be known that he wanted company and everyone had obediently attended. He did not mind that the guests did not stay long—he had his own private plans for the latter part of the evening—but was satisfied that they came and made obeisance. The sudden passage into professional oblivion of those who had ignored such invitations in the past was a permanent warning to others.

Not a great deal had happened. People had gone through the usual pantomime of expressing the correct levels of admiration and envy at things they had seen before—personal messages on framed photographs of pop stars, the guitar bearing the autographs of all four Beatles and their Svengali manager Brian Epstein—and had assured Barry that everything about him was marvellous. All their contempt, hatred and fear had been smothered in sycophancy. Almost certainly, Barry Kershaw had been aware of the hypocrisy, but had not been concerned; he had been the East End kid—legitimate by birth, bastard by nature—holding court as glitterati of London's Sixties paid homage. The girl could not think of anyone who would mourn when they heard he had been found dead, his sly, avaricious face smashed and bloody; there was more likely to be an outbreak of celebration parties. She was startled out of the satisfying thought by the telephone ringing on the table beside her. She hesitated then picked it up.

"Hello?"

"Is Barry there? It's John Knight from the *Daily Sketch*."

"No . . . he's gone out." The girl found the grotesque literal truth of the statement amusing.

"How long will he be?"

"Quite a while I think." Another grim smile.

"Have him call me when he gets in, will you? Tell him it's urgent. OK? He's got the number."

"I'll tell him. John Knight you said?"

"Yeah. He'll know what it's about."

"All right. Goodbye."

"Just a minute . . . who is that? Don't I know you?"

"I don't think so. I'll give Barry the message. Ciao."

She rang off before he could ask any more, then, shocked into reality as the sick humour of her replies evaporated, walked back to the balcony windows and looked across streetlights stretching down Edgware Road towards Marble Arch. Suddenly one of those illogically preserved fragments of childhood came back to her and she remembered looking through the window of her parents' home, yellow cornfield at the back of the house imprinted almost photographically on her mind. Indelible recollection, held like perfect flies in amber in some corner of memory, triggered a flood of other chance-held incidents; her father planting a rose bush next to the garden bird-table, mother overjoyed at that new evening dress, her sister hesitantly pedalling her first tricycle down the garden path. Why did so many immaterial events that the mind inexplicably recorded seem to have happened on summer days? Perhaps memory did not hold on to winter so well. Stung by the contrast of lost innocence after all that had happened since, the girl wept.

When she recovered, she sat down and began to think more calmly. The last guests had left sometime after eleven o'clock—it was now half-past midnight. Had they realised she was still there? Probably not. She had been in the loo when she heard them go and they had been half drunk anyway. Nobody knew that she had let Barry know she was prepared to spend the night with him after diplomatically refusing for so long. When the police came there would be fingerprints and countless other indications of her presence, but that was the same for all the rest. The journalist's phone call would reveal that someone had been in the flat after the party ended, but although he had thought he recognised her voice too many cigarettes had made it unnaturally husky; if he had been certain, he would have said so immediately. She convinced herself nobody would ever realise that she had been the only witness to the moment when the web of Barry Kershaw's empire had been broken. All the crooked agents and bent lawyers who drew up loaded contracts, the paid-off journalists and tame thugs, had lost their master spider. She smiled bitterly as she deliberately dropped her cigarette and ground it into the carpet with the toe of her boot; Barry would have gone mad at that. Then she left.

Bird-song was busy in the early morning air when a milkman found the body. At first he thought it was a drunk who had passed out on the way home, but then he saw the crude star pattern of rust-brown stains framing the shattered head and ran back into the road, bottles clanking noisily in their metal carrier in the silence, and leapt into a phone box. The news spread so rapidly that the first celebratory bottles of champagne were being opened almost before the body had reached the mortuary. Three weeks later, after the inquest at which so many people lied, Barry Kershaw's body was cremated. Years afterwards, when they began writing the history of the Sixties as legend, he did not even rate a footnote, but those who had been dominated, used and destroyed by him never forgot. Neither did the one person in the world who loved him.

Chapter One

"Which is the order of monks who never speak?" Tess Davy asked idly. "I've forgotten."

"Trappists," Augustus Maltravers replied from behind *The Guardian*. "Although there is a legend that they sing very beautifully just before they die."

He lowered the paper and looked across the breakfast table at the morning image only he ever saw. Long, burnished-bronze hair ragged as a mass of bracken catching late May sunshine filling the kitchen, pale skin unlit by make-up, slender figure wrapped in a shapeless candy-stripe housecoat. It was the reality behind the groomed and sparkling actress the public knew, when the hair gleamed like dark flame and witchcraft-green eyes could conjure up any human emotion. With the vanity of her profession, Tess only allowed the man she loved to see her without the mask of cosmetic deceit.

"Why do you want to know?" he added as she scribbled in the margin of the *Daily Mail*.

"It's a competition. We could win a country hotel weekend break in the Cotswolds."

"Sounds nice. How do monks come into it?"

"It's in conjunction with the publishers of something called *The Ultimate Trivial Pursuit Answers Book* so it's fairly eclectic." She considered the rest of the questions. "What was Doris Day's real name, what's the capital of Liechtenstein and who was King Arthur's father? I should know that one as well."

"Doris Kappelhof, Vaduz and Uther Pendragon." When Trivial Pursuit had been all the rage, Maltravers's ragbag mine of useless information, accumulated by voracious reading since his youth and years as a journalist, had made him tediously unbeatable. "Any more?"

"No, I've got the rest." Tess dropped the *Mail* on the floor and picked up the *Daily Express*. She devoured all the morning papers, amused by, if disbelieving, the gossip, alert for anything that might be professionally useful and simply keeping in touch with the world in which her audiences lived. Flicking through the pages, she paused and peered closely at a picture.

"She's worn well."

"Who has?" Maltravers asked, mind again absorbed by a Surrey v Yorkshire match report.

"Jenni Hilton."

His reaction surprised her. Instantly putting down his own paper, he stretched his hand across the table. "Let me see that."

For a few moments he looked at the picture, frowning as though trying to remember something.

"Better than well," he corrected. "She's even more beautiful."

"More beautiful?" Tess regarded him with interest. "Is there something about your past you haven't told me?"

"Not really." He smiled nostalgically. "I was once madly in love with her, that's all."

"Really? You've kept very quiet about it." Tess firmly took the paper back and examined the picture more critically. "I didn't know I had predecessors like that."

"You didn't. It was a hopeless passion. She was incredibly famous and I was a sixth former with fantasies."

"Fantasies?" Tess repeated teasingly. "Were they very dirty?"

"'Tread softly, for you tread on my dreams,'" Maltravers warned her. "It was all very juvenile, but don't tell me you didn't have teenage crushes. In fact, didn't you once lust after somebody's older brother? Jason something wasn't it?"

Tess shuddered. "Pax. Double pax. I still feel embarrassed whenever I see someone on a Norton motor bike. I even forced down halfs of beer for him. And he had spots."

"Then don't knock me and Jenni Hilton. I can't have been the only one besotted with her in those days." He shook his head in disbelief. "God, it's more than twenty years ago."

"We were so terribly young, dahling." Tess's voice dropped a couple of octaves and she dramatically grasped his hand across the table. "Now we are old and wise and have found true love."

"But are still susceptible to a passing motor bike or a newspaper photograph. Let's see the story." Tess handed the paper back and began to clear the table as he read the Diary page item.

Among the guests at last night's première of Tom Conti's new play, who should I spot but Jenni Hilton who has hardly been seen anywhere since she walked out of a film in 1968 and disappeared.

For those of you who have forgotten, she was one of the biggest names of the Sixties, scoring four number one hits before switching to acting, winning an Oscar nomination for her part in The Stuart Queen.

I tried to speak to her as she was leaving the Albery, but la Hilton was being as elusive as ever. However, I understand she has now returned to live in London. She was alone and there was certainly no sign of the sort of gorgeous escorts who squired her in the old days. What a pity. As you can see, the lady is still very lovely.

"Do you remember her?" Maltravers asked as he finished reading.

"Hardly." Tess had done the washing up—two cups and two plates for toast; breakfast was always minimal—and was drying her hands. "I've seen her films on TV—she was very good—but I was very little when she was very big. How old is she?"

"Four years, three months and six days older than me," Maltravers said. "I worked it out. When you're seventeen, that's a lot."

"And when you were seventeen, I'd have been six," Tess added. "I was heavily into Beatrix Potter, not pop singers."

"Don't know why you stick around with an old man."

"I'm after your money."

"I don't have any money. I'm a starving author."

"But with life insurance and a two-bedroom flat in Highbury."

"Highbury and Islington," Maltravers corrected.

"If you're selling, you don't mention the Islington. And I'll be selling." Tess ruffled his hair as she crossed the kitchen. "In the meantime, I'll have to keep working. I'm due at the studios at eleven."

"Oh, yes, it's that voice-over job where you play a soap bubble. Fine thing for a legitimate actress."

"It's paying a hundred pounds an hour and it's going to be a major television campaign," Tess called back as she left the room. "The repeat fees will be worth a bomb. If it's good enough for Judi Dench, it's good enough for me."

"She doesn't play soap bubbles," Maltravers shouted after her.

"I'm not a Dame and I don't play Cleopatra at the National. Now get off your butt and do some writing."

Maltravers picked up the post—three bills, a Reader's Digest special offer and a royalties cheque which was not going to change his life—and took it to the front room where his desk stood in the bay window overlooking Coppersmith Street. He had bought his flat when he started on Fleet Street in the 1970s, appalled at the price compared to his native Cheshire and the Midlands where he had worked immediately before. But what had cost him fifteen thousand pounds was now comfortably into six figures. He was in the not uncommon position among Londoners of his generation, sitting on a piece of real estate worth a fortune and constantly hard up. Since he had abandoned full-time journalism for the precarious life of a writer of plays and novels, supplemented by freelance newspaper features, his income and cost of living had remained as close to each other as horses in a photo-finish. But with Tess's earnings, they managed to remain vaguely solvent. To all intents and purposes, they now lived together, but she had kept her own flat in Muswell Hill which brought in extra money through short-term lettings to other actors who needed a temporary base in town. If they married, they could sell both properties and afford . . . but marriage had fallen into the background. Sensing that Maltravers still had residual hang-ups from his first experience, Tess had wisely stopped even joking about it. The result was that one of their friends had described them as the most married unmarried couple she knew.

He loaded a disc into his word-processor and lit a cigarette as the machine muttered to itself before throwing a menu on the screen. He called up the third chapter of a new book and read through what he had written the previous day, correcting mistypings and deleting a passage afflicted by chronic adjectivitis. He rapidly wrote three more paragraphs and immediately wiped them out. The cursor blinked at him, an agitated green sprinter waiting to be sent dashing across space leaving deathless prose in its wake. A milk float rattled to a halt outside and Maltravers watched the milkman until he drove up the street. He contemplated deep crimson flowers on the tree *paeonia* by his front gate, reflecting that he had never got round to cutting out the dead wood, waved to a passing neighbour, craned his neck to see if the curtains at number seventeen had been opened yet—they had been closed for three weeks and he and Tess were becoming intrigued—and finally took a copy of his first novel from the bookshelf next to the desk, opening it at random to persuade himself that what he had done before he could surely do again. Finding several passages he would have rewritten given the chance, he dropped the book on the floor, put his chin in his hands and stared at the screen as though willing it to inspire him. All it did was wait. After a few moments he crashed his mind in gear and began to write flat out, letting words flow without interruption by analysis; an eventual salvageable ten per cent of something was going to be better than a hundred per cent of damn all.

By the time Tess reappeared, elegant in yellow silk blouse and burgundy suit, he was absorbed, grunting vaguely as she kissed the top of his head and left. An hour produced more than a thousand words before he ran out of steam and went to make a cup of coffee; as he returned, the telephone on the desk rang.

"Gus? Mike Fraser. Glad I've caught you. Can you do an interview for us?"

"How much?"

"Don't be so mercenary. It's supposed to be a privilege writing for *The Chronicle*."

"Privileges butter no parsnips and I've got parsnips gasping for butter. And do you realise you're interrupting great art here? We could be talking Booker Prize country."

"Then you'll expect us to review it, so be nice to me."

Maltravers was joking and Fraser, features editor of *The Chronicle*, knew it. In the three years since the paper had been founded, it had established a reputation for quality writing and Maltravers was flattered when his work appeared in the same columns as the likes of Alan Bennett and Anthony Burgess.

"All right, you've talked me into it," he said. "What is it?"

"An interview with Jenni Hilton. Remember her?"

"Not only do I remember her, Tess and I were talking about her only this morning. Have you seen the piece in the *Express*?"

"Glanced at it." Fraser sounded dismissive. "Snatch picture outside the theatre and a caption story cobbled-together at the office. We've got something better than that lined up. Are you free?"

It was a ludicrous question. At one period of his life, Maltravers would have fought dragons for the chance of simply being in Jenni Hilton's presence; while such idiotic passions had now mellowed, the possibility still excited him. He would have been prepared to do it for nothing, but was not going to let Mike Fraser know that.

"When does it have to be done?" he asked.

"Soon as you can. She's expecting to hear from you."

"Me specifically?"

"You specifically."

"But I've never met the woman."

"Ah, but she . . . hang on a minute." Fraser broke off and Maltravers could hear him talking to someone else. "Gus, the boss wants me. Come to the office at lunchtime and I'll fill in the details over a beer. OK?"

"Fine. About twelve thirty?"

"Look forward to it. Cheers."

Fraser rang off and Maltravers replaced his own phone thoughtfully. The coincidence of Jenni Hilton reappearing in his life twice in one morning was irrelevant; the fact that he was being offered the chance to interview her—and that she apparently wanted him to do it—was much more interesting. There was no question of their having met, even fleetingly, at some theatrical party with Tess—he would never have forgotten that—so how did she know about him? Perhaps she had seen one of his plays or read one of his books? Could it be that after all these years she was now a fan of his? He tried to return to his work, but was deflected by a ridiculous sense of anticipation, feelings which he had dismissed as the embarrassing excesses of youth more potent than he would ever have expected after so many years. He eventually gave up, leaning back in his chair and remembering.

Jenni Hilton had been an icon of the Sixties. Gazelle-thin, height exaggerated by long slender legs in mini-skirts and chestnut hair falling water-straight to her waist. Those wide lips would have been a disaster on another face, but in her case only accentuated disturbing beauty. Locked in solid rings of mascara, the eyes seemed never to blink, dark pools of brown flecked with shreds of gold. She had started as a pop singer, smoky voice adding depth to lonely ballads, before emerging as a different animal from the endless parade of discoveries with a half life of about a month. For Jenni Hilton had revealed an intelligence and level of articulateness which set her apart. Chancing to see her in conversation with a distinguished philosopher on some television programme had first caught Maltravers's attention; his musical taste committed at the time to the MJQ, Dave Brubeck and Brahms, the Top Ten hardly interested him, so he had been only half aware of Jenni Hilton from hearing records played by his friends. Suddenly there was this girl, lovely beyond description, discussing Voltaire and John Stuart Mill; as this occurred at a time when Maltravers was becoming aware that there might possibly be more to women than mothers who complained about the state of his room and a younger sister who slammed doors a lot, he was vulnerable and was captivated. The picture of England's opening batsman on his bedroom wall was replaced with a large coloured poster of Jenni Hilton and he dreamed dreams.

Already beyond his reach, she had risen further, dazzling as Viola in *Twelfth Night* on television, and shattering in a film of the life of Mary Tudor. There had been more films, including *Madam Bovary*, a commercial failure, but still remembered by many as a portrayal of Flaubert's tragic heroine which tore a human soul bare. As he thought about it, Maltravers was caught again by the agonising death scene, the screaming woman on the bed intercut with flashbacks to writhings with her lovers. And after that . . . nothing. Half-way through the filming of something called *Tiger Lily*, Jenni Hilton had vanished. Agitated producers threatened to sue her—if they could find her—close friends were evasive, less close ones baffled. Sensing all manner of sensation, Fleet Street's finest were set loose, coming back with stories each designed to top the fevered imaginations of their rivals. She had gone mad (*Daily Sketch*); she had contracted leprosy (*Daily Mail*); she had entered a convent (*The People*); her body had been dragged from the Thames (*Evening Standard*) or found strangled in a lesbian lover's flat (*News of the World*); she had been kidnapped (for some extraordinary reason, *The Sunday Times*). Out-of-focus pictures put her in Stockholm, an Indian village in Brazil, even—the unforgivable sin in a Cold War climate—standing next to Fidel Castro in Cuba.

By the time she did reappear—alive, sane, healthy and not a terrorist—living in California, nearly ten years had elapsed and she was almost *passé*. Polite but firm refusals to be interviewed damped down any spluttering flickers of renewed interest and Jenni Hilton, while not quite as hermit-like as Garbo, was definitely no longer public property. And now she was back in London and prepared to talk to a national newspaper. Prepared, more to the point, to talk to Augustus Maltravers.

"But what did you run away from?" he murmured aloud. Once acquired, a reporter's instincts to smell an angle and pursue it are never lost. He picked up the telephone again and rang *The Chronicle*'s cuttings library, explained what he had been commissioned to do and arranged to call in for some background information before he met Mike Fraser. There had been something connected with Jenni Hilton's sudden disappearance which he could not drag out of his memory banks, and he wanted to find out what it was.

Chapter Two

Between two and three million readers saw the *Express* Diary piece about Jenni Hilton. Many ignored it completely, some glanced at it briefly, others for varying reasons responded to it. Members of a generation now middle-aged found the picture conjured up memories of back-combed hair piled in beehive domes, adolescent rows with their parents, tacky first flats away from home, gauche experiences of sex beyond the *frisson* of stocking tops. They remembered the daring spurious sophistication of rum and Coke and steamy coffee bars with gushing stainless steel Espresso machines where they had sat for ever, solving all the problems of the world except their own confusions. Faded stars who had vaguely known her felt again yesterday's glamour, the dazzle of flashbulbs, excited fans, the lights and chaos of television studios which they had not been in for a very long time. Approximately thirty men, married more than fifty times over the years, recalled going to bed with her; several others felt they might have done, but could not be sure. A number of women bitterly resented the fact that nature had been kinder to Jenni Hilton than to them and one had vivid memories of screaming obscenities at her then husband in a hotel bedroom where he was not spending the night alone; it did not seem very important now.

And one woman was obsessed, reading the report over and over until she could have quoted it word for word, staring intently at the picture, noting the natural elegance that even a hastily snatched photograph could not miss, the grace of a woman who had gone from dazzling youth to mature loveliness and who would never be less than beautiful. And a hatred that had never stopped smouldering began to inflame. London was not as big a city as many people imagined, the original villages it had swallowed up over centuries close neighbours. Jenni Hilton would not be living out in the suburbs which sprawled for miles, but within a limited area: say Notting Hill to the west, Hampstead to the north, possibly Docklands to the east, although that part of London had been slums in her time; probably not south of the river, which had only been fashionable in the Sixties once you reached stockbroker Surrey. The likely area was limited, but dense with terraces, courts, squares, mews, cul-de-sacs, streets hidden off main roads unknown except to their residents, studio and basement flats, penthouses and luxury apartments, hotels, secret houses hidden behind high walls. But she would find her. If Jenni Hilton went to the theatre once, she would do so again; her reappearance would excite attention. However private she wanted to be, there would be more paragraphs in the papers. It was only a question of time, and she could wait a little longer.

The features department of *The Chronicle* appeared to have been furnished through an office supplies firm offering a discount on anything in red. Scraps of paper bearing illegible scribblings littered the surfaces of interlocking plastic units; books sent in by optimistic publishers waited to be either thrown out or taken home by somebody; stacked filing trays overflowed with press releases which had achieved a permanent condition of pending; notes scrawled on yellow labels clung from their adhesive strips to computer screens waiting for their users to arrive. Standard works of reference—*The Oxford Dictionary for Writers and Editors*, *Who's Who*—lay alongside a couple of disintegrating dictionaries and Roget's *Thesaurus*.

On the walls were faded travel posters, a seventeenth-century map of Clerkenwell and a portrait of Elvis Presley circa 1960 advertising shoes. Banks of filing cabinets, crowned by piles of bound official reports, were accumulating into a serious fire hazard; above, a silent television tuned into the BBC's Ceefax service hung suspended from steel arms. From stain-blotched grey carpet tiles to ceiling strip lights—several not working—there was an air of untidiness. Behind the disciplined order of how news is presented to the public lies a perpetual mild chaos.

Sometimes the disorder erupts into panic when the usually repetitive pattern of newspaper life is disrupted by a major late-breaking story, but the rule is that if you can keep your head while all about are losing theirs, you have obviously not grasped the situation.

Not that there was any air of panic as Maltravers walked in at twenty past twelve. The soft plopping of electronic keyboards as features were checked, cut and polished by sub-editors gave the room an atmosphere almost as restful as the ancient City of London graveyard the first-floor windows overlooked. Telephones which had once rung with strident urgency now uttered a discreet soprano bubbling tone, so much more easy to ignore if you were busy. Engrossed in the text filling his screen, Mike Fraser was sipping hot chocolate from a white plastic cup as Maltravers walked up behind him and looked over his shoulder.

"Must be a good piece," he commented.

Fraser turned round and made a face of distaste. "It's by someone we pay a fortune for a weekly funny column. I've had more laughs out of a Christmas cracker motto, but he's a friend of somebody's wife." He stood up and held out his hand. "Good to see you, Gus. How do you keep looking so bloody young?"

"Clean living."

There was less than three months' difference in their ages, but Maltravers had once said that Mike Fraser had been thirty years old when he was born. His swarthy face looked as though it had been lived in carelessly, seamed with lines that suggested harrowing experiences; a broken nose, legacy of violent years as a rugby forward, added a touch of menace and dark tan hair was short and tough as a doormat. But the appearance was totally deceptive. Mike Fraser had been married for more than fifteen years to a delicate and outrageously pretty Japanese wife and was father to two daughters who had inherited their mother's looks and their father's warmth. Maltravers was one of the few people who knew that he was a volunteer with his local branch of the Samaritans. If Mike Fraser was tired when he arrived for work, it was probably because he had spent half the night on the telephone sympathetically listening to someone on the verge of suicide, and usually talking them out of it.

"Find what you wanted in the library?" he asked as he put on his jacket.

"It filled in some details," Maltravers told him. "I certainly didn't know she was living in Wales a couple of years ago. The most recent item was a par in *The Guardian* about some row over a nuclear power station. How long has she been back in London?"

"Not sure. Only a few months though."

"And how did *The Chronicle* get on to her?"

"The editor met her at a dinner party. She said she liked the paper and he talked her into an interview."

"And why me?"

"Remember that piece you did for us about Richard Tomlinson? The playwright? He's a friend of Jenni Hilton from way back and she was very impressed with the way you handled it." Fraser grimaced cynically. "Said you were sympathetic."

"And is it a case that she'll only do the interview if it's with me?" Maltravers asked casually.

"Oh, no," Fraser told him firmly. "Don't try that angle to jack up your fee. She's quite prepared to talk to somebody else if you—"

"I'm sure we can sort something out," Maltravers interrupted. "Over a drink. Offer me enough and I may even buy them. Where are we going?"

"The Volunteer," Fraser replied as he logged off from his screen. "I must introduce you to Dame Mary on the way."

"Who Dame Mary?" Maltravers asked.

"You'll see. It's worth the detour."

They left the office and walked up the City Road to the gates of the neighbouring graveyard. A flagged path ran straight between tombstones decaying beneath beech, sycamore and plane trees. Just before they reached the opposite gates, Fraser turned right towards an imposing box tomb with the information that it contained Dame Mary Page, relict of Sir Gregory Page, Bart, carved on one side.

"Now look at this," Fraser said. "It's one of the unknown delights of London." Maltravers followed him to the other side and read the legend in silent amazement.

In 67 months she was tap'd 66 times. Had taken away 240

gallons of water without ever repining at her case or fearing the operation.

A martyr to the dropsy, Dame Mary had spent the last five years of her life drowning from the inside but, despite endless discomfort and indignity, had endured it all with saintly fortitude and a stiff English upper lip.

"Wonderful isn't it?" Fraser commented.

"One of the classics," Maltravers agreed. "But have you ever wondered where they buried normal people? I'll guarantee that everyone in this place was either a perfect wife and mother, upright and faithful husband or a child on temporary loan from the angels."

"Death cancels all debts."

"Maybe, but I want to find a gravestone with something like: 'She was a constant embarrassment to her family, drank like a fish, beat the servants, made her husband's life hell and God is welcome to her.' "

"That the sort of thing you want?"

"I shan't be buried, but if I was I'd leave strict instructions for them to put something along the lines of . . ." Maltravers paused. " 'He was no worse than many and at least some people liked him.' "

"Very philosophical. Come on, let's drink to it."

Dwarfed beneath modern office blocks, the Volunteer retained its dark Victorian splendours; polished mahogany square central bar, wooden partitions set with stained glass, immense framed mirrors bearing the names of past breweries in faded gilt. Wallpaper swirling with wine-dark vines ran nearly twenty feet up to a ceiling with an ornate plaster ornamentation in the middle, empty now of the massive chandelier which must once have hung from it. The pub was packed, full of the chatter of young City whizz kids who could earn more in a day than the original customers had made in a lifetime. Fraser waited to be served at the bar as Maltravers made his way round to the other side of the room, squeezing past a man with a portable phone telling his wife that something had come up and he would be delayed, possibly to the extent of having to stay in town overnight. As he spoke he kept smiling at a girl standing next to him. Maltravers noted sensuous mouth and body, and charitably concluded she must be his niece. Fraser appeared through the crush carrying the drinks, and they found themselves what passed for a quiet corner.

"Let's assume that you say two fifty, I want five hundred and we settle for three fifty," Maltravers suggested amiably. "Cheers."

Fraser sniffed. "Twist my arm and we'll make it four hundred. It's for the front of the Weekend section, so we're looking for about two thousand words. We'll decorate it with a new pic of her and perhaps some sort of Sixties montage."

"God bless you, sir, you have a lucky face," Maltravers said. "An unlucky body, but a lucky face. Any particular line you want me to go on?"

"No," Fraser replied. "Just a profile piece as deep as you can make it, although I think you'll find there are some no-go areas . . . She gets to read your copy before we publish, incidentally."

"You're joking!" Maltravers protested. "I haven't had to do that since I was a weekly reporter. What clown agreed to that?"

"The editor—it was the only way he could persuade her to talk," Fraser said. "But don't worry. She can only correct any errors of fact. How you write it is up to you."

"I check my facts before I hand my pieces in."

"Like you check your manuscripts?" Fraser inquired mildly. "In your first novel you had someone driving around in a 3.7 litre Bentley. There's no such thing."

"All right, so I'm not good on cars," Maltravers admitted.

"You're bloody awful. Come on, Gus, any of us can make a mistake in copy. She won't be able to change anything unless she can prove you've got it wrong. Of course, if you can't accept that, we can always . . ."

"No, I'll live with it," Maltravers said. "Just don't change anything without letting me know."

"No problem," Fraser agreed. "So when are you going to see her? She's in town for the next couple of weeks, but then she'll be away for a few days."

"When do you want it by?"

"Soon as you can."

"Well, I can start whenever you want," Maltravers said. "All I need is the address."

"Twelve Cheyne Street. Do you know it?"

"I know the area," Maltravers confirmed. "Royal Borough of Kensington and Chelsea in that slice of London between Hyde Park and the Thames. Very upmarket. Phone number?"

"It's in the office. Did the library throw up anything useful?"

"There was one thing." Maltravers took out a notebook and began flicking over pages. "I half remembered it, but the details had gone . . . here it is . . . About a month before she vanished, Jenni Hilton was a witness at the inquest of some character called Barry Kershaw. He was mixed up in the pop music business as a fixer or agent or something like that. Threw himself off the top floor of a block of flats. Suicide. Ring any bells?"

Fraser shook his head. "Never heard of him. Was he famous?"

"There were some big names at the inquest. He certainly knew a lot of famous people."

"And what are you thinking? About Jenni Hilton?"

Maltravers shrugged as he put the notebook away. "Nothing specific. But his death and her disappearance were close together. I smell a possible angle, but I'd like some more information before I see her."

"From that far back?" Fraser looked thoughtful for a moment. "Most of the people from those days are dead or gaga now . . . Unless . . . What the hell was his name? News editor on the old *Daily Sketch*. Everybody knew him . . . Tom Wilkie."

"Tom Wilkie?" Maltravers repeated in disbelief. "He must be a hundred and eight! Where is he?"

"Newspaper Press Fund retirement home in Dorking. I was talking to someone the other week who'd been down to see him. Still has whisky with his cornflakes every morning—and still has a mind like a steel trap apparently. He was giving chapter and verse on the Profumo affair and how he scooped everyone with some exclusive on the Great Train Robbery. If you want to know about anything that made news between the end of the war and 1980 when he retired, he'll tell you. You do remember him, don't you?"

"Who could forget?" said Maltravers. "He once tried to poach me from the *Daily Mail*. In the back bar of the Harrow just opposite the office it was. Christ, he could have given Bacchus drinking lessons. Damned good operator as well."

"Then he's your man. If this Kershaw was news, Tom will probably be able to tell you everything including his shoe size. Try calling him when we get back."

Their conversation was interrupted by the arrival of two other members of *The Chronicle* staff. Maltravers had never met either of them, but within minutes they discovered mutual acquaintances in the remarkably small village in which journalists live. For the next hour, Maltravers let himself be absorbed again in the world of legendary cock-ups, unforgettable—often unforgivable—characters, gruesome misprints and incidents like the weekly newspaper in Yorkshire which put out a billboard in 1912 reading, "Titanic Disaster: No one from Cleckheaton drowned". Journalists are finally story-tellers and very good at a little polishing to improve the facts where necessary. It makes them excellent company—and keeps libel lawyers off the streets.

Things were busier when they returned to the office, a couple of hours nearer deadline prompting the thought that there seemed to be more work to do than there was time left for its completion. Fortified with four pints, Fraser went back to his unfunny funny columnist and Maltravers rang the Newspaper Press Fund, the charity founded by Charles Dickens which looks after journalists who have not prepared for the day when their monthly pay packets stop; this includes virtually all of them and most do not even have the foresight to join the fund. A life lived in daily or weekly bites does not lend itself to long-term planning. It was likely that Tom Wilkie had signed the membership forms when he was out of his tree one night and forgotten all about it, so he had never cancelled. So, probably by mere chance, he was now being fed and watered in the company of his own kind. Maltravers was given the number of the Dorking home and called it. Yes, Mr Wilkie was there. If he would just hold for a moment . . .

"Wilkie." Glaswegian Gorbals toned down to be comprehensible to English ears still had the snap of a Black Watch sergeant major.

"Hello, Tom. Gus Maltravers."

There was a short silence, then, "*Daily Mail* about 1975. Tall, brown hair, blue eyes, thin face. Kept using long words in your copy but could crack a story all right. Turned down a job I offered you on the *Sketch*. Married Fiona West from the *Sunday Mirror*. Right?"

"What was my mother's maiden name?"

"Piss off," Wilkie said. "How's the business?"

"Much the same. No new stories, they just happen to different people. I'm only on the edges these days, anyway. I quit to be a writer."

"Better than ending up on *The Guardian* like you wanted to."

"Cynic. Look, Tom, I need some help with a piece I'm working on. Do you remember someone called Barry Kershaw?"

"Full back with Aston Villa who turned out to be queer?" Wilkie had always considered "gay" a prissy euphemism. "Great story, that."

"No, another one. Mixed up with the pop business in the Sixties. Committed suicide by—"

"Killer Kershaw?" Wilkie interrupted. "What's brought him up again?"

Maltravers scribbled down "Killer" and underlined it several times. "It's just a possible line on a feature I'm doing. Why killer?"

"He had a habit of wrecking people's careers if they stepped out of line. I'll give you a quote I got once which never made it into print. 'The stench of Barry Kershaw makes vomit smell like roses.'"

"Who said that?"

"Jenni Hilton. Remember her? There were a couple of pars in today's *Express* about . . . Hey, what are you on to?" Imperishable news editor instincts surfaced again.

"Possibly nothing," Maltravers replied. "I'm just kicking around some ideas. Why did she say that?"

"Because he was a shit," Wilkie told him bluntly. "Everybody said the same sort of thing, but hers was the best quote. We were working on an exposé at one time, but the lawyers put the mockers on it and the next thing he was dead."

"Suicide," Maltravers repeated.

"You don't question coroner's verdicts."

"And what am I supposed to understand by that?"

"You're on the story and I'm an old man," Wilkie said. "Nobody remembers Kershaw now, except burnt out buggers like me. But I'll give you a contact. Louella Sinclair. She'll know as much as anyone."

"Where do I find her?"

"Shop on the King's Road called Syllabub. Can't remember the number, but it's towards the Sloane Square end. I know it was still there about six months back, because I was driven past it."

"What were you doing in town?"

"They wheeled me out for another bloody memorial service at St Bride's." There was a faint Scottish melancholy which Maltravers had never heard before in Wilkie's voice. "I have to look in the deaths column in *The Times* every morning to make sure I'm still alive. Nearly all my generation's gone now. About time I did as well."

"You'll live for ever, Tom," Maltravers assured him. "Now I know where you are, I'll come down sometime. Promise. And I'll bring a bottle. Glenmorangie, twelve years old, isn't it?"

"When I moved in here, the doctor said it would kill me."

"How long ago was that?"

"Nearly ten years." Wilkie chuckled wickedly. "Mind you, the doctor's dead. That was one funeral I didn't mind going to."

Chapter Three

Jenni Hilton knew that the interview with Maltravers was the first bridge she had to cross. As Russell had grown older, she had found it harder to dismiss the constant comments from friends regretting she was not using her talents. Now he was at university and she was a free agent again. She had needed the years of fiercely-protected privacy, but the idea of a comeback had become increasingly insistent. Her career had mattered, the demands it had imposed stretching her and giving a sense of being her own person, unique and separate from the child she had been. Part of her personality had become under-nourished, not by lack of fame which was meaningless, but by an intangible feeling of dissatisfaction, almost waste. It had nothing to do with money. She had made a great deal during more than five years of success—even now royalties trickled in—and it had been intelligently invested. Her father had been a successful career diplomat and Jenni and her sister had jointly inherited nearly half a million pounds on his death. Money had never been important—it was just there—but the intellectual challenge of everything she had run away from was missing and she began to want it back.

She had spent a long time thinking about how she might accomplish a carefully controlled return. Publicity would be part of the price, a loss of safe anonymity. Agreeing to talk to *The Chronicle*—a newspaper far removed from the hysterics of the tabloids which had once pursued her like hungry wolves—was the first step. But she was still meeting a journalist again and was out of practice at evading the apparently innocent but loaded question, cautious of everything she said in case some phrase could be maliciously extracted out of context and distorted into a different meaning. In the Sixties, she had rapidly learned how to play the game, now she was only accustomed to being with people she could trust who did not lay traps for her unguarded tongue.

Her misgivings were alleviated when Maltravers telephoned from *The Chronicle* offices and they talked for nearly half an hour, although his initial inquiry had been nothing more than to arrange a suitable time to see her. He had self-mockingly confessed his teenage infatuation before perceptively discussing her film performances. His knowledge of acting techniques led to the revelation that he had written plays and had an actress girlfriend.

"You don't sound like a journalist," she had commented at one point. "At least, not the ones I've known."

"There are some tame animals in the zoo," he had replied. "One of the reasons I quit it full time was that I wasn't prepared to bite people hard enough."

She felt less uneasy about it after agreeing to see him in a couple of days. A call to Richard Tomlinson, the playwright Maltravers had also interviewed for *The Chronicle*, gave further reassurance. Tomlinson told her about Maltravers's reputation—far from a bestselling writer, but admired by those who knew his work—and said he had respected the confidentiality of certain things he had been told. Jenni Hilton accepted that he could be something she had not believed existed; a journalist who did not threaten. In that he was rare rather than unique, but her experience had been almost exclusively restricted to those who would never let the facts get in the way of a good story. It did not occur to her that he might not be prepared to let anything get in the way of the facts.

As Maltravers opened the front door in Coppersmith Street, a high, squeaky voice greeted him from the direction of the front room.

"Hello. I'm Bubbles. Shall I show you what I can do to all those horrid dirty dishes? Just watch *this*."

He stepped across the hall and stood in the doorway. Tess was holding a very large Scotch—it was only four o'clock—and had a glazed look of total insanity on her face.

"See?" she squeaked hysterically. "They're so shiny and sparkling you can see your face in them."

"Come on, you're making it up."

Tess shook her head. "I couldn't make it up. Nobody could. When I read the script I nearly walked out. But I'd signed the sodding contract and was stuck with it. I did it in five different voices and I'm just praying to God they don't decide to use my real one."

"Think of the money."

"Think of the shame." She swallowed half the whisky. "Anyway, never again, unless I get to read the script first. I found your note incidentally. *The Chronicle*'s asked you to do an interview?"

"Yes, but not any old interview," Maltravers told her. "Jenni Hilton, no less."

"Jenni Hilton?" Tess sounded intrigued. "The love of your life?"

"You are the love of my life . . . Bubbles," he replied. "And don't start taking the piss again or I'll make sure everyone knows your secret."

Tess grinned and kissed him. "I'm not taking the piss. It's marvellous. How did it happen?"

She stretched out on the settee as he told her about the afternoon, including the line on Barry Kershaw that he wanted to investigate, and his call to Tom Wilkie.

"You're going to see Louella?" Tess sounded unexpectedly delighted. "I'll come with you."

"Do you know her?"

"I haven't seen her for ages, but I must have spent a fortune in Syllabub. I may spend another while you're talking to her."

"What's she like?"

"She's . . ." Tess paused and gazed at the ceiling. "Incredible. If you put her in a book nobody would believe you. When are you seeing her?"

"I was going to try ringing her now and fix it up for the morning."

"Tell her you know me and that I'll be with you." Tess stood up. "Now I'm going for a shower . . . with no bloody bubbles."

Ten minutes later Maltravers put the phone down and went through to the bathroom.

"We're seeing her at about half-past ten," he said to the outline of Tess's body behind the shower curtain. "Odd call, though."

"In what way?" Tess asked above the splash of the water.

"Can't quite explain it. It was as though she was startled at being asked about Kershaw. Frankly, I think if I hadn't mentioned you she'd have said no. She sends her love, by the way."

The water stopped and Tess pulled the curtain back. "It must have surprised her being asked about someone who died that far back. Pass the towel."

"There was more to it than that." Maltravers took the towel from the wooden rack and handed it to her. "It was almost as though she was frightened."

"Nobody frightens Louella Sinclair," Tess said firmly as she began to dry herself. "She frightens them. You'll see what I mean."

"I simply *refuse* to let you walk out of here with that, madam! The colour's not you, the style is out of the question on forty-inch hips and we're not eighteen any more are we? In fact, I think we've passed it twice and the second time's fading into memory isn't it? If there's nothing on the rail over there, there's a little place down the road doing a very *bijou* line in tents. The colour range is limited, but the dimensions are generous."

Tess raised an amused eyebrow as Maltravers stared at her in silent disbelief. Fighting time and weight, the customer did not appear in the least offended, but was obviously appalled at the prospect of being forced to leave empty-handed. Bitchy insults from the proprietor were clearly part of the price one paid for patronising Syllabub, on top of labels that started in the low hundreds. The wait had also been an opportunity for him to observe Louella Sinclair; high heels, close-fitting grey skirt and white frilly blouse with a cameo brooch at the throat. Mustard-gold hair, long and expensively tousled around a square and determined face, could have been a wig, but it was impossible to be certain. Poised, sleek and confident among pastel water-colours, William Morris wallpaper and subtle lighting, she worked on the principle that the customer was invariably wrong and had to be told so. It was an approach which very few retailers could get away with. The woman obediently moved to the rail which might enable her to purchase something from Syllabub—two others had already been bluntly turned down as unsuitable—and Louella Sinclair was free to talk.

"Sorry to keep you waiting, but one of my regular girls is off and the stand-in staff simply don't know how to handle some of these women." Dark brown voice was edged with masculine notes. "They'd sell to anyone who walked in waving a Coutts chequebook around. Tess, you're looking marvellous."

She kissed her then stepped back holding both her hands, expertly assessing the combination of Jacques Vert skirt and blouse. "Not absolutely right with your hair colouring, but infinitely better than some of the horrors I see."

Tess bowed slightly in acknowledgement and Louella Sinclair turned penetrating slate-blue eyes towards Maltravers. "And this is the man who wants to talk to me about Barry Kershaw, is it? Can I trust him?"

"Yes you can, Louella," Tess told her. "Completely."

Louella Sinclair held out her hand and Maltravers felt the grasp of strong fingers capped with ox-blood nails. "We'll talk in private."

She led them through the shop and into a small room at the back. Such unseen facilities were usually tatty and undecorated, but here the chairs and the table on which freshly made coffee was waiting were quality Georgian reproductions and two Hockney prints hung on the wall.

"Please sit down." She picked up the silver pot. "It's Cuban, but surprisingly good. And do try one of these." They accepted Fortnum and Mason truffles and she began to pour the coffee. "Before I say anything at all, I want to know something. What's brought Barry Kershaw up again?"

"Chance," said Maltravers. "His name cropped up when I was doing some research into Jenni Hilton."

"And why were you doing that?"

"I'm going to interview her for *The Chronicle*. Did you know her?"

"At the London première of *The Stuart Queen* she borrowed

my lip gloss in the ladies room. That was as close as we ever got, although I often met her casually here and there. But I thought she took a vow of silence donkey's years ago."

"She's about to break it. She's moved back to London again as well."

"I'd heard." Louella handed them their cups then sat on a shield-back armchair. For a moment she sipped her coffee in silence.

"I need an assurance from you right from the start," she said finally. "Nothing is to be written down and I want your word that you haven't got a tape recorder hidden in that jacket. Agreed?"

"I haven't," Maltravers assured her. "Tess will confirm that I don't cheat."

"If you hadn't told me you knew Tess, I don't think I'd have agreed to see you at all," she replied. "Incidentally, how did you find me?"

"Someone called Tom Wilkie said you knew Barry Kershaw. You might not recall him, but he was a Fleet Street news editor in those days and still remembers just about everything and everybody."

"Well, I don't remember him. But there were so many journalists and general hangers on . . . God, it's so long ago now. All right, let's see how we go. I'll start by telling you something about myself."

White fluted china cup and saucer were gently replaced on the table and a minute crumb of truffle brushed off the skirt, then Louella leaned against the arm of the chair, hands clasped together. "I was a student at the Royal College of Art in the early Sixties. Fashion was all the rage and I was attracted to it. I was never going to be a star, but I could take anything the designers came up with and perfect it. I began picking up freelance work, which was marvellous when you were starving on a grant, and was eventually offered a job which was so good that I left college without completing the course. My boss was Hilly Janes—totally forgotten now, but she really was one of the greats—who made exclusive outfits for virtually all the pop stars of those days. I became part of the scene, and that's how I met Barry Kershaw."

Mentioning the name again appeared to trigger recollections. A flash of distaste crossed Louella's face before she continued.

"He was a very interesting man in his way. He came from nothing—his father was a docker in Wapping when it was still an East End slum, not part of yuppieland like today—but he had an amazing capacity for work and a genius for seeing what or who was going to be the next temporary sensation. He was also very, very nasty. He knew exactly how to manipulate people, discovering their weaknesses and exploiting them ruthlessly."

"When you say nasty, how exactly do you mean?" Maltravers asked.

"He was . . ." She rubbed her hands together as though trying to remove something from them. "For a start, he was a sadist and I mean that literally. I never had first-hand experience of his sex life, but there were girls who told me some very sick stories. And it went further than that. Humiliating people gave him a kick. I have never met anybody who was so utterly devoid of basic human feelings. He didn't have an ounce of kindness in him. I don't think he understood the word."

"But he was successful," Maltravers repeated.

"Very," Louella confirmed. "London was full of groups and singers trying to make it in those days and Barry would go to the most awful clubs to check them out. If he thought someone had potential, he would present himself as Mr Fixit—which in fairness he was. They were so grateful at the chance of a break that they'd sign contracts which were as rigid as death warrants. He milked them dry during their fifteen minutes of fame then threw them away. If they became really successful and could afford lawyers to challenge the contracts, he made sure it cost them a fortune—and then destroyed them. Do you remember a group from the Sixties called Jack's Spratts?"

"Only vaguely. I was more a modern jazz fan in those days."

"Well, they were very good. Jack Buxton was a great bass guitarist and very talented composer. You still hear them on golden oldies shows on Radio Two. Anyway, they had two number one hits in a row and were obviously going to be very big. Jack realised that their contract with Barry would mean him ripping them off for ninety per cent of their earnings for ever and managed to get a court to overturn it. Barry received some compensation, but the word was out that you could escape his clutches if you fought hard enough."

Louella paused. "A few weeks later, Jack was picked up by three men outside his flat. They bundled him into a car and took him to some house or other where they worked him over . . . Do you know how many bones there are in your hand?"

"No. But it's quite a lot isn't it?" Maltravers suddenly felt uncomfortable about where the conversation was leading.

"About twenty-five in each one." Louella looked straight at him. "They broke all of them with a hammer, right hand and left. Jack passed out with the pain and the next thing he knew he was lying on the pavement where they'd dumped him outside Guy's Hospital. Considerate in a sick sort of way. He never played the guitar again."

"Louella, that's dreadful!" Tess protested. "Are you saying that Barry Kershaw was behind it?"

She laughed sourly. "Oh, my dear, Barry had left for the Bahamas a week before it happened. Jack received a grotesque bunch of flowers from him with a letter saying he'd read about it in the papers out there and how horrified he was."

"Was he suspected?" Maltravers asked.

"Of course he was. The police even questioned him, but he simply denied it and they couldn't prove a damn thing. The men were just hired thugs and probably didn't know who they were doing the job for. The police never traced them."

"But you think Barry Kershaw arranged it."

"I *know* he did. We all knew. And if he could do that to someone as big as Jack Buxton, he could do it to anybody."

Maltravers took out his cigarettes and looked inquiringly at Louella for permission. She nodded and pushed a smoke-blue cut-glass ashtray across the table, but refused when he offered her one.

"Who else did Kershaw handle?" he asked.

She shrugged. "Quite a lot of people, but they came and went so fast that I can't remember many of them now. Jack's Spratts were the biggest group and there was a singer called Tony Morocco—he was really Tony Ramsbottom, but that had to be changed—who bore a faint resemblance to Tom Jones and sounded like Mario Lanza on a bad day. He really was appalling. He had a couple of hits then sank without trace like most of the others. Barry lost interest when anyone stopped making money."

"What about Jenni Hilton?"

"No." Louella shook her head firmly. "Jenni was originally discovered by Stephen Delaney who was a record producer with Decca. Later he became her manager. Lovely man. He died of Aids about a year ago."

"So what connection did she have with Kershaw?"

"If you were in the music business, there were things you just did," she explained. "Adam Faith—or was it Mike Sarne?—said that a lot of male singers were homosexual for reasons of business or pleasure. Your agent told you it would be a good thing to attend this party or be nice to that person and you did it. Barry's circle spread very wide and a lot of people became part of it, if only temporarily."

"That's too vague," Maltravers told her. "Can you remember anything more definite between them?"

"Why do you want to know?"

"Because Jenni Hilton gave evidence at his inquest and vanished only a few weeks later."

"Are you saying there was a connection?"

"No. It may have been nothing more than coincidence, but it's worth looking into from where I'm standing."

"Then I'm afraid I can't help you. As far as I know, Jenni Hilton and Barry Kershaw were just two people who had a common background of pop music."

"But she was at his party the night he died," Maltravers said.

"So were a lot of others. Including me."

Maltravers noticed that Louella Sinclair looked away as she spoke and had the feeling he was entering delicate ground. He finished his coffee. "What happened that night? Anything you remember particularly?"

"Not really," Louella replied. "Barry had put the word out that he wanted company and there was no question of anyone refusing. We drank and listened to some music. Fawned over Barry. I left about ten o'clock with a friend. The next morning someone rang me with the news that they'd found him dead."

"I've read the inquest report," Maltravers commented. "He jumped off his balcony when he was high on LSD. Obviously thought he could fly."

Louella Sinclair's caustic "Yes" smothered the word with cynicism.

"Yes, what?" Maltravers asked sharply.

"Yes he was high on LSD," she replied simply.

"And?" Maltravers pressed. "Or but?"

"But Barry never took LSD. Or any other drug."

Maltravers frowned. "But at his inquest, people said—"

"People lied," Louella interrupted. "Exactly as I would have done if I'd been called. Before the inquest, we heard that the police had found LSD in his body and everybody realised someone must have tricked him into taking it."

"And nobody at the party told the police that?"

"Of course not. If they had, heaven knows what sort of trouble we'd all have been in. Anyway, we were more inclined to give whoever had done it a medal than turn them in. It only needed enough people to say that Barry was a part-time addict to provide the perfect cover story."

"Who for?"

"I don't know and I don't think anybody does. The night Barry died there must have been forty or fifty people wandering through his flat. It was all very casual and nobody could say who was or wasn't there when they left. But one, perhaps two, people would finally have been left with Barry on his own. He'd have been fairly drunk and the LSD could have been given to him without any problem. Then they'd just have had to lead him on to the balcony and say, yes, Barry, you really can fly."

"And you believe that happened?"

"I can't think of any other explanation."

"Who'd have had access to LSD?"

She looked surprised. "Just about everyone. It was almost as common as a pack of cigarettes in that set."

"Did you have access to it?"

"Of course. I even tried it once . . . but I didn't give it to Barry. I wasn't clever enough to think up something like that."

"Who do you think might have been?"

Louella shrugged. "Any one of a dozen people, but I can't see any way of finding out who it was now."

Maltravers leaned forward to stub out his cigarette. "So everybody closed ranks, the witnesses lied about him being a drug addict . . . and nobody said what you're now telling me? Didn't he have friends who must have realised what could have happened and went to the police?"

'First of all, Barry Kershaw didn't have any friends," Louella said. "A lot of people knew him, a lot of people hated him, a lot of people were frightened of him. But nobody liked him—apart from his family."

"And what did they do?"

"His mother was at the inquest," Louella replied. "Ghastly woman who kept interrupting when people were giving evidence. The coroner nearly had her thrown out. She insisted that Barry never took drugs. She was right about that, of course, but she also had to admit that his life had become almost totally separate from hers, so her evidence didn't carry much weight. Frankly, I think the coroner wanted to believe that Barry took LSD. He made some standard caustic comments about declines in moral standards. We didn't like it, but it suited what everyone was saying."

"But you say the LSD story wasn't true."

"No." She sipped her coffee. "Barry Kershaw could get hold of drugs and he supplied them to other people—it was another way of controlling them—but he despised their weakness. 'Drugs is for mugs' was his favourite line, and whatever else he was, he wasn't a mug."

"So . . ." Maltravers hesitated ". . . you're saying it was murder?"

"Either that or a joke that went badly wrong."

Maltravers leaned back in his chair, looking at Louella Sinclair thoughtfully. She did not strike him as being either fanciful or likely to suffer from hyper-imagination; she had told the story of a possible murder as calmly as someone reading out the ingredients of a recipe.

"Go back a bit," he said. "You say that before the inquest the word was out that LSD had been found in his body. Who said so? It's not the sort of thing the police would have announced."

"I can't remember exactly where I heard it now," Louella admitted. "Everyone was talking about his death of course and the story just got around."

"But at that stage, the only person—or people—who'd have known were whoever gave it to him," Maltravers pointed out. "So they'd have been the only ones who could have spread the story. This is starting to sound like a plot, Louella."

"Possibly, but I don't think so—at least not if you mean that murdering Barry and covering it up was planned by a number of people. I'm positive I'd have picked up something if that had been the case."

"But once the LSD story came out, everyone went along with it and backed it up, either by giving evidence or not saying anything," he observed. "*That* was a plot."

"You could call it that," she acknowledged. "But it wasn't organised. It was just an unspoken agreement between us all."

"An unspoken agreement to lie at an inquest? With all the risks of being prosecuted for perjury if they were found out?" Maltravers sounded sceptical. "Come on, Louella, that's heavy."

"I'm still certain that's what happened and a lot of people would agree with me," she replied levelly. "If you'd known Barry Kershaw, I think you'd believe it as well. He wasn't just disliked, we loathed him. Let me put it this way. When Barry held a party, we all turned up; when he died, nobody who knew him attended his funeral. They burned him at Golders Green crematorium and his family were the only people there. I was at a party in Bayswater that afternoon and it was like New Year's Eve. We counted the seconds, shouting them out until the moment we knew the ceremony was due. Then we cheered and laughed and danced and got tremendously drunk."

There was a silence as Maltravers and Tess absorbed what she had said. It was a rare and ugly achievement to have been so hated.

"Was anyone taking drugs at Barry's party?" he asked.

"A couple of people were smoking pot, but that hardly counted. It wasn't that sort of evening. It was come when you want, leave when you want—just make sure you came or Barry might notice you weren't there and feel offended. And you didn't offend Barry."

"And that afternoon in Bayswater," he added. "The day of his funeral. Was Jenni Hilton there?"

Louella shook her head. "No. I'm sure of that because I remember meeting her the following day and telling her about it. I think she'd been out of town filming." She raised a plucked eyebrow questioningly. "You're surely not thinking she had anything to do with it are you?"

"You said anyone could have given him the LSD," Maltravers reminded her. "Are you including Jenni Hilton?"

"Jenni would never have done it," Louella insisted. "I've told you there was no special connection between them as far as I know. They hardly knew each other."

"Then if she wasn't particularly close to Kershaw, why was she called as a witness and, according to you, lied about his drug taking?"

Louella pursed her lips and glanced at Tess. "Doesn't miss much, does he?"

"No, he doesn't," Tess confirmed. "And what's your answer, Louella?"

"I don't know. You're quite right, there were plenty of people who knew Barry much better. I've never really understood why she gave evidence."

"How about she knew who'd done it and put herself forward to protect them?" Maltravers suggested.

"It's as good a theory as any," Louella agreed. "Are you going to ask her about it?"

Maltravers stared at one of the Hockney prints without replying. When he had confirmed that Jenni Hilton's unexplained disappearance had come so soon after Kershaw's inquest, his professional antennae had locked on to a possible angle, but he had thought it nothing more than that she had been distressed over the death of a friend. That was now obviously not true. When Fleet Street had been trying to find her, at least two reporters had mentioned Kershaw in their stories but had not turned up anything significant. He half remembered a quote from somebody to the effect that she had hardly known Kershaw and had only been at the party by chance. But now he was being told of a conspiracy of silence after his inquest, protecting not only a killer, but also the witnesses who had lied to damn a man they all hated.

"I'll need to think about that," he said. "Asking someone if they were an accessory to a murder isn't the sort of thing you can just casually bring into an interview. And I've been told she's laid down some rules, like no questions about her private life. Tricky."

"And does it really matter?" Tess asked. "If Louella's right and Barry Kershaw was murdered, he sounds as though he deserved it. Even if Jenni Hilton was mixed up with it in some way, it's been a sleeping dog for more than twenty years. Is it any of your business?"

"No," Maltravers acknowledged. "But it's one hell of an angle."

Chapter Four

Echoing through Tottenham Court Road Underground station, someone was playing 'Body and Soul' on tenor saxophone, the melody faintly audible on the westbound Central Line. Across the track, the blown-up image of a minimally-dressed brunette, sprawled in a pose suggesting constant availability, imaginative enthusiasm and inexhaustible sexual energy, stared challengingly. The caption read: WHAT THE AU PAIR WILL BE WEARING THIS WINTER. Virtually every man waiting for the next train had looked at the picture and read the slogan, but none had registered what was being advertised. Dotted orange lights on the platform indicator showed "Ealing Broadway 2 mins" and "West Ruislip 5 mins". Among the crowd of more than a hundred passengers, tourists anxiously checked maps to convince themselves they had their directions right and were not about to be carried out to unknown Ongar or Epping instead of Bond Street or Lancaster Gate. Most, however, were going through a familiar, repetitive early-evening routine. Some read their papers, others talked, voices gathering into a hum of sound beneath the arched roof. Most just waited.

Distantly, from out of the black hole at one end of the platform, came a muffled rumble and an unpasted corner of the au pair poster trembled as a faint draught of air began to flow. People instinctively moved forwards as the indicator blinked to "Next train approaching". The rumble grew louder and the draught stronger. A copy of a giveaway magazine which had dropped on to the track fluttered then was swiftly blown along between the rails. The rumble rose to a roar and lights appeared in the black throat of the tunnel, then the long concrete cavern was filled with the crashing rattle of the train, carriage after carriage pouring out of the tunnel's mouth.

Suddenly a scream of terror screeched through the racket and a man leapt back as he was splattered with human blood; a woman standing next to him whirled round and vomited. At the centre of the platform there was panic, passengers further along turning towards shouts of horror at the sight of a human body mangled beneath steel wheels. In the confusion, people stared at each other helplessly. An off-duty ambulanceman went to attend a woman who had fainted. Somebody hurried away to tell the station staff. The train driver scrambled out of his cab, shouting as he pushed through the crush. Several regular commuters simply walked away, mentally working out alternative routes home.

Within two minutes, two uniformed policemen hurried down the centre escalator of the three leading to and from the main entrance, bundling passengers out of their way; people rising in the opposite direction wondered what had happened. Among them was one woman who looked at the police indifferently before disappearing in the crowd passing beneath the mosaic tiled arches at the top. She went through the ticket barrier and along the green and cream tiled corridor to the steps that led out into Oxford Street, emerging by the newspaper stand opposite McDonald's. She ignored a girl handing out leaflets for courses in English and walked along the busy pavement towards Marble Arch then turned into Soho Square, with its anachronistic mock-Tudor arbour in the middle of the gardens. She cut through to Dean Street, past advertising agencies, film companies, the Chinese News Agency and the Sunset Strip until she reached the Groucho Club. The girl at reception was on the telephone, but smiled in recognition as she entered through the revolving door and signed the members' book. In the bar, she was greeted by several people. A man asked what she wanted to drink and she said a vodka and lime; in the Groucho, that automatically meant a double. As the woman sat on the brown, buttoned-leather settee by the window, somebody pointed out a small dark stain on her skirt. She glanced at it, then rearranged the material so that it did not show.

"Spaghetti sauce," she said dismissively. "I had lunch at the Vecchia and the waiters were as mad as ever. It'll wash out." Nobody noticed that the stain wasn't dry.

Overlooking the arrow-straight reach of the Thames between Chelsea Bridge and Battersea Bridge, Cheyne Walk is a good address. The view from its Queen Anne houses across to Battersea Park costs a great deal; Cheyne Row, Place, Mews and Gardens are acceptable for those who can't have the real thing, but, hidden away from the river, Cheyne Street is the poor relation, anything under a million pounds or so for a property being bargain basement price in that neighbourhood. Its mirror-image Edwardian terraces of twelve houses on each side are functional rather than elegant, with spearhead railings rising on either side of three front steps and ornate glass lanterns over the doors. Maltravers made his way there by bus—a form of transport unknown to most of the residents—as even his knowledge of London would not be able to locate a parking place within miles. Discovering he was early, he walked down to the river and along the Embankment before turning up Flood Street, marked for minor historical fame as once being the home of Margaret Thatcher.

The ridiculous anticipation of meeting Jenni Hilton was still with him, but now there were unexpected dimensions. The dramatic recluse could also have been involved in a murder to the extent of lying . . . and more than that? The thought that could not be dismissed as unthinkable returned again. He deliberately walked more slowly, turning over in his mind how to approach it. At first there would be no more than an arranged interview and, while they talked, he might be able to build up enough of a rapport for them to chat generally afterwards. Perhaps she would accept an invitation to lunch. Journalists meet all sorts of people in all sorts of circumstances and putting on whatever act is necessary to win their confidence is a trick they learn early. Maltravers had his own writing and Tess's career with which to build bridges and was quite prepared to use them. It was not completely honest, but that was not a recommended virtue when digging out difficult angles on a story, and this angle was uniquely difficult.

As he entered Cheyne Street, he realised he was mentally checking his appearance and was annoyed at such juvenile behaviour. But standing outside Jenni Hilton's door, he felt again memories of teenage excess, its emotional traces more vivid than common sense. It was ridiculous. He reminded himself that since then he had enjoyed an affair with a model who was now among many men's fantasy women and had a permanent relationship with another glamour figure in Tess. Behind fame and beauty were women like millions of others without make-up in the morning, bed was not the be-all and end-all, friendship mattered more than sex and . . . Christ, she was lovely. Logic temporarily collapsed as the door opened and Jenni Hilton was smiling at him.

"Gus Maltravers? Hello. Come in."

Tapered black trousers looped beneath feet in flat shoes; white cotton shirt hanging loose at the waist with a designer logo on the breast pocket; large costume jewellery earrings shaped like a boat's sails; long hair pulled back off her forehead and held in a ponytail; make-up so subtle as to be almost invisible and fingernails gleaming with silvery lacquer.

"'Splashed with a splendid sickness, the sickness of the pearl,'" he said as they shook hands. What a stupid thing to say, he told himself.

"Pardon?" she glanced down and laughed. "Oh, the nails. Nobody's ever been poetic about them before. Don't tell me . . . Chesterton isn't it? Lepanto?"

"Yes." Maltravers felt like someone discovering that the Taj Mahal really was as unbelievable as it looked in pictures; Jenni Hilton talked his language. "I had a girlfriend about a hundred years ago who used something similar and I used to quote it to her."

"God, I must be out of date." She smiled again. "Coffee's ready in the front room. You're very punctual."

"After waiting twenty-odd years to meet you, I could at least be on time."

"Don't flatter," she warned as he followed her down the hall and into the front room. "I stopped falling for that journalists' trick a very long time ago."

The front room was basically as it had been when the house

was first built. An old-fashioned wooden picture rail still ran round the walls and the black marble fire surround with mock-classical pillars and mantelpiece had been left in place. Instead of ripping such things out, Jenni Hilton had used them as a framework for carefully selected contemporary furnishings: Montpelier painted bureau, Meubles Français dining suite, William L. Maclean sofa. Muriel Short fabric curtains, vivid with scarlet flowers, were offset by pale cream Regency striped wallpaper. It was the room of a woman with taste and the money to express it. Maltravers mentally took it all in—selected mention of certain touches added depth to an interview—and at the same time firmly stamped on his feelings and switched his mind into detached, professional gear as Jenni Hilton poured coffee from a prosaic glass percolator jug.

"I thought of getting out the proper coffee set, but the cups really are too piss elegant," she said, filling him a plain white mug. She sounded slightly mocking.

"And too good for scruffy journalists?" he remarked.

"Oh, dear." Now she sounded surprised. "Are we offended? Reporters don't normally have thin skins. Sugar? Or are you sweet enough?"

"Two, please," Maltravers replied. "And cream." He watched her spoon sugar into his mug. He had anticipated she might be defensive, but had not known how; obviously needling antagonism was being used and he would have to deal with it.

"I was told you'd put down ground rules for this interview," he said as she handed him the mug. "Let me set my stall out as well. There are many journalists who make me as sick as they do you, but I don't operate like them. You asked for me and now you've got me. You'll find out how straight I am when you read my piece and it's going to make life easier if you come out from behind your barriers."

She pursed her lips thoughtfully. "Prepared speech?"

"No. Instinctive response to a couple of oblique cracks. I'm not sensitive, but I am upfront."

Jenni Hilton smiled. "I think you are and I'm sorry. I've been . . . very nervous about this morning. Apology accepted?"

"Of course. It's perfectly understandable."

"Do you want to go out and come in again?"

"No need to go that far." Maltravers grinned at her. "Hey, aren't you Jenni Hilton? I used to be crazy about you. Can we talk?"

A grin flashed back to him. "You want an autographed photo?"

"Will you sign it 'With love to Gus'?"

"I never put 'love'. But you can have 'Best wishes'."

"And a kiss? I really want a kiss."

"Don't push it." She laughed and held up her hand in surrender. "All right. It's just that I wasn't nervous about this, I was getting shit scared. I haven't done this sort of thing for a long time."

"You'll survive." Maltravers produced a pocket tape recorder and put it on the low table between them. "Let's see how we go. If any of my questions get too awkward, just tell me and I'll turn this thing off and we'll talk off the record."

She shook her head in disbelief. "You mean that, don't you? How the hell did you hold down a job on Fleet Street?"

"Your problem is over-exposure to the worst of my kind," he replied. "We don't all kick the door down and lie through our teeth."

Jenni Hilton settled back in her chair. "Show me."

Maltravers had won the opening gambits and began his interview with basic questions, to which he already knew most of the answers, but they started her talking and he could sense her relaxing as they proceeded. She was objectively critical about her own work and shrewd in her assessment of the Sixties and its personalities. If anything, the tape was picking up more good lines than he would have space for; some people can talk for hours and the journalist later despairs of finding a single sentence worth using verbatim, others have a natural ability with words. Now cynical, now sympathetic, always articulate, Jenni Hilton emerged as the best sort of subject; she spoke in quotes. Only when he reached the reasons for her own sudden disappearance did she show signs of evasiveness. Maltravers cautiously led up to, and for a while stepped around the matter carefully, but eventually she shook her head abruptly.

"Turn it off," she told him. "This doesn't matter."

"Sorry." He pressed the stop button on the recorder. "I'm

going outside my brief a bit, but you must admit it's interesting. Not many people give up a career such as you had just like that."

"Perhaps not, but the reasons are personal. OK? I'm quite prepared to talk about some of the things I've been doing since, and if you want my opinions on the fur trade or North Sea pollution I've got plenty of soap boxes I stand on. But why I quit is off limits."

"Fine." Apparently disinterested, he turned the machine on again. Instinctively, he felt it was not the moment to mention Barry Kershaw. "I've picked up your trail in California and Wales. What were you doing there?"

Not a great deal as it transpired. Having accumulated money, Jenni Hilton had lived a private life bringing up her son—his father's identity was not going to be revealed—and doing some writing, none of which had been published. She had returned to Britain so that the boy could go to school and, now that he was in his first year reading medicine at Exeter University, had returned to London.

"And what about a comeback?" he asked. "It's long overdue."

"It . . . has its attractions." She had always intended using the interview to trail her coat and see if it brought any reaction. "Not singing, but I'd certainly be tempted to act again if the right part came up."

"I must try and write one," Maltravers said. "Anyway, I think I've got everything I want. If I come across any gaps, I'll phone you."

He smiled at her as he turned the recorder off again and put it back in his pocket. "Thank you. Wasn't too bad, was it?"

"I've known worse . . . no, that's attacking again. Let's say that several teeth were extracted quite painlessly."

"I'm glad," he replied. "Now, it's personal request time. I really was a fan—that wasn't just a line to win you over—and I'd love to buy you lunch so we can just talk. No tricks. Everything from here on in is off the record."

"Well, I could pretend to have an engagement, but . . ."

"But you haven't."

"'What can a neat knave with a smooth tale make a woman believe?'" she quoted, challenging with her eyebrows.

"If Tess was here, she'd confirm I'm rather good at that game," he said. "Webster, *The Duchess of Malfi*. Anyway, where do you suggest? This part of town is outside my usual hunting grounds."

"There's a decent wine bar just off the Embankment. Give me five minutes."

She left the room and Maltravers heard her go upstairs. He had discovered that the real Jenni Hilton was as attractive to him in much more subtle and satisfying ways than the unreachable star figure had been and just to spend more time in her company would be a pleasure. But there was still Kershaw's death hidden in one of the no-go areas of her life. How he was going to explore it he had no immediate idea, but having overcome her initial antagonism and built up the beginnings of a willingness to trust during the interview, he decided to mention Kershaw's name casually over lunch and see what happened. Perhaps he would hit another blank wall . . . but perhaps he would draw blood. Twenty years earlier, he would have been tongue-tied and gauche in Jenni Hilton's presence. But not now.

Chapter Five

"Hello, this is the Gus Maltravers and Tess Davy mansion. Nobody's about at the moment, but if you're a burglar checking out the premises the only things worth stealing are the two Rottweilers. Otherwise leave a message after the traditional tone and we'll call you back. Please remember to give your name and number to save us guessing. Thank you for calling and have a nice day if you're American. Or British come to that."

"Oh . . . Gus, it's Louella Sinclair. I'm sorry, but something's happened that . . . There's a story in last night's *Standard* about a woman killed on the Tube. Page two. She was a very good friend of mine and . . . look, I'll be at the shop until six and after that I'll be at home on 228 0142. Call me as soon as you can."

Louella Sinclair's eyes returned to the paper lying open on the table by the telephone as she rang off. It was the first edition, carrying news which had broken too late for the West End final the previous day. She had bought a later edition to see if they had enlarged the story, but there had been nothing more than the same three paragraphs under the headline HUNT FOR TUBE DEATH WITNESSES.

Police have named a woman who was killed when she fell under a Central Line train at Tottenham Court Road yesterday as publisher Caroline Owen of Sheppard Gardens, Holland Park.

Mrs Owen, 50, who ran Scimitar Press, in King Street, Covent Garden, was identified from the contents of her handbag. She was married to Ted Owen, chairman of the advertising agency

Owen Graham Metcalf, although the couple are believed to have been separated.

Her death is being treated as accidental, but a police spokesman said: "The incident occurred during the rush hour and we are sure that some people on the platform left before the police arrived. We want anyone who witnessed the incident to come forward."

The original story had been longer. Inquiries among her neighbours had established that Caroline Owen had lived alone since her marriage had broken up and little was known about her private life; Scimitar Press published children's stories and books on organic gardening and cookery. Off the record, the police had said they felt that probably somebody had stumbled against her in the crush as the train came in and had panicked when they realised what they had done. There certainly appeared nothing to suggest suicide. A new reporter, anxious to impress the News Desk with a front page exclusive off the police bulletin, had failed to turn up anything. He had padded out his copy as much as possible, but a sub-editor with only six centimetres of space for the story and headline, had chopped it down to the bare essentials. One fact had not emerged because it was so obscure; Caroline Owen had been at Barry Kershaw's last party in 1968.

Shocked at the news of a friend's death, Louella Sinclair tried to analyse instinctive, irrational, feelings. Logically, it was no more than coincidence that she had been talking about Barry Kershaw so recently. And the conversation had inevitably started her thinking, remembering people who had been involved, wondering again what had really happened. Common sense told her that she'd read stories before of people dying on London's Underground. Some fell by accident, others deliberately chose to end their lives in such a desperate, bloody and certain manner. But others could be pushed. It was such a simple method of killing somebody. Surrounded by dozens of potential witnesses, but all watching the train, only interested if it would stop with doors conveniently facing them. There would be subtle jostling as people manœuvred themselves into better positions, but there was a tendency not to look at anyone around you. One firm hand in the back of someone already half moving forward, then panic, a leaping away, confusion, screams. Any number of people could slip away, one guilty invisible among the innocent. Unless the police discovered a motive, it was a perfect murder covered by the explanation of tragic accident.

Think, Louella, she told herself. Suicide was out of the question; it was only a couple of weeks since Caroline had been round to dinner, excited about a new author, talking about finding time for a holiday at the end of the year, joking about changing her hair style—"Tell me it won't look ridiculous, darling. I'm not *that* old"—simply happy. So not suicide, but a terrible accident, just like the police were saying, and it was stupid to start imagining that . . . The door of the back room opened.

"Lady Penelope's here, Miss Louella."

"Thank you, Emma. I'll be out in a moment."

Louella Sinclair took a deep breath and forced a smile at the mirror on the wall in front of her. A Duke's daughter buying new spring outfits had to be given all her attention, but over the next two hours, during which she sold three thousand pounds' worth of clothes, she never completely stopped thinking about Barry Kershaw and Caroline Owen.

"Do you remember Louella Sinclair from the old days?" Maltravers asked casually as he poured the last of a bottle of Chablis into Jenni Hilton's glass. Lunch had been a success, all her guards down as they had talked about the theatre, music and films and had laughed together at the manners of the Sixties, so daring and vibrant when they had lived them, slightly quaint and mannered as the Twenties now that they had also passed into history.

"Louella Sinclair?" She frowned. "I don't think so. Should I?"

"Not necessarily," he replied. "She was one of what must have been an awful lot of people milling around. Worked in the fashion business for someone called Hilly Janes."

"Oh, I remember Hilly Janes. She made an absolutely gorgeous dress that I wore for the Hollywood Oscars ceremony.

I've still got it somewhere. Couldn't possibly wear it again, but there was no way I was going to throw it out. But I can't remember this Louella person. Why do you ask?"

"I met her the other day. She owns a dress shop on the King's Road—only a few minutes' walk from here—and Tess is one of her customers. I was taken along to provide the credit cards. It came out that I was seeing you and she mentioned that she used to know you." There was enough truth in the explanation to make it a seamless lie.

Jenni Hilton shrugged. "Well, I might recognise her if we met, but I can't place her."

"A few other names came up as well," Maltravers added, producing his cigarettes. She accepted one and he leant across the table to light it for her. "There was someone called . . . Larry, or . . ." the lighter flicked a couple of times before igniting, ". . . Barry Kershaw."

It was only because he was so close and watching carefully that he saw the fleeting reaction. Dipped towards the flame, the cigarette momentarily trembled and alarm darted through her eyes and was gone. Maltravers lowered his face to light his own cigarette, apparently indifferent.

"Barry Kershaw?" Smoke was inhaled and expelled, then she coughed slightly. "Sorry, they're stronger than mine. No, I can't remember him, either. Anybody else?"

Maltravers turned away and caught the waiter's eye, gesturing with a scribbling motion across his palm that he wanted the bill. "Can't recall all of them. People I'd never heard of. Don Currie was one, I think. And . . . Lindy Sharpe?"

His mind was racing as he randomly threw out the names of a couple of journalists he knew. Jenni Hilton might not remember Louella Sinclair, but it was unbelievable that she should have forgotten Kershaw; she had been a witness at his inquest. So she was lying. He moved away from the subject as though it was irrelevant.

"Anyway, Louella asked me to send her love," he said. "Look, this has been absolutely marvellous, but I'm not going to overstay my welcome. Thanks for the interview. I understand they've agreed to let you read it first. Frankly, I'm not over the moon about that, but went along with it because I wanted to meet you. If there's anything you're not happy about, could you call me direct so we can sort it out?"

"At the office?"

"No. I'm a freelance don't forget. I'll give you my home number." He found an old petrol receipt in his wallet and scribbled on the back of it. "There you are. I never seem to get around to having cards printed."

"I don't imagine there'll be any problems." She put the slip of paper into her bag. "I'll be interested to see how you handle it."

"Can I walk you home?"

"No thanks. I want to do some shopping and . . ." She paused as the bill arrived and Maltravers put thirty pounds on the plate, indicating that the balance could cover the tip. "I'd like to thank you as well. You've made it much less painful than I thought it would be. Now I've only got to worry about the photograph tomorrow."

"That's no problem," he assured her as they rose to leave. "*Chronicle* photographers win awards all over the place. Just relax and let whoever it is get on with it."

They parted on the pavement outside the wine bar, Jenni Hilton to go up to the King's Road and Maltravers to walk back along the Embankment. He could have gone with her part of the way, but wanted time to think. She had lied about Kershaw so smoothly that he was convinced she had anticipated his name coming up and was prepared for it. What would she have said if he had challenged her with what he knew—and why hadn't he? Because after talking to Louella Sinclair, he was not sure what he was dealing with and wanted to tread carefully. For the time being he had all the material he needed for his piece and, if she liked it enough, Jenni Hilton might agree to see him again. Perhaps for dinner with Tess when he could . . . He watched a pleasure boat on its way up river to Hampton Court, the sound of the amplified commentary distantly audible across the water against the background rumble of traffic.

". . . our left is Battersea Park. Colonel Blood hid in the reeds on the bank when he was planning to shoot Charles II in 1671 and in 1829 the Duke of Wellington fought a duel here with Lord Winchilsea. All very gentlemanly; they both deliberately fired wide. Today the annual veteran car run to Brighton starts in the park. Ahead is the Albert Bridge, originally built by R. M. Ordish in 1871–3. It is curious in that it is both cantilever and suspension. Beyond the bridge you can see . . ."

Fragments from London's chequered history faded and the waves of the boat's wake sloshed against the Embankment below where Maltravers had stopped. Why had she lied? Don't know, but think it through. She must have realised he had done his homework; enough had come out during the interview to show he had checked out her past. Therefore she should have guessed that he would have unearthed Barry Kershaw and her connection with him. So lying had been stupid, which was totally out of character. She should have admitted knowing Kershaw and produced some story to explain it away—but explain what away? Maltravers walked past the grounds of the Royal Hospital, his mind ferreting for explanations. His instinctive knowledge of London north of the river—on his mental map, anywhere south of the Thames, apart from the National Theatre, was marked "Here be dragons"—took him through Pimlico and past Victoria Station and he only consciously became aware of where he was again when he reached Grosvenor Place. He contemplated options for a moment, then walked to Hyde Park Corner, through the underpass and along Piccadilly to catch a Victoria Line train at Green Park. He saw a newspaper placard reading TUBE DEATH WOMAN NAMED, but took no notice. By the time he reached Highbury and Islington, the only certainty he had come up with was that Jenni Hilton must know that her lie had been inept and suspicious. So what would she do? What would he do?

Do nothing. He could have been telling the truth about being told Barry's name by chance. He had not pressed it, and surely no journalist would leave something like that alone if they knew anything. But he wasn't like other journalists she had met. They were cunning but clumsy; he was intelligent—and disarmingly charming. It was easy when you could see how their sordid minds were working, but he had been much more subtle . . . subtle, false and treacherous? Staring blankly at supermarket shelves of vegetarian dishes, Jenni Hilton felt she had been fooled, her vanity flattered by a handful of quotations. He had smoothly manœuvred her into a corner over Barry Kershaw—and then backed off. Why? Because he had not realised what he had done? Possibly, but she could not rely on that . . . Who was the woman he had mentioned? Louella Sinclair, and she had a shop somewhere nearby. If she'd worked with Hilly Janes, it was almost certain to be an upmarket dress shop—but which one on the busy King's Road? Would it help if she found it? Did Maltravers know anything else which he had not mentioned? How dangerous was he? Suddenly he had made the risks of coming out into the open again appear very real.

"Is that you?"

"No, it's a pickpocket who stole my keys." Maltravers went through to the kitchen where Tess was at the sink, scrubbing new potatoes. "Who were you expecting?"

Tess twisted round and nodded towards an open copy of the *Evening Standard* on the table. "Look at the bottom of page two. Louella left a slightly panicky message about it on the ansaphone."

Maltravers read the story in seconds. "Christ! Caroline Owen!"

"Do you know her?"

"She used to be my editor. She was working for my publishers when I wrote my first novel, but left a few months after it came out. I went to her launch party for Scimitar Press."

"Oh, darling, I'm sorry." Tess turned from the sink in dismay. "I didn't realise she was a friend of yours. Have I ever met her?"

"I don't think so. I haven't seen her for God knows how long, but she gave me a lot of help when I was starting and we got on very well. We used to have lunch from time to time. What did Louella say about it?"

"Just that she wants you to ring her."

"And she sounded panicky?" Reading the story again, Maltravers walked towards the door.

"Certainly agitated, but she didn't say why."

The girl who answered the phone at Syllabub first of all said that Louella was with a customer, but when Maltravers mentioned his name to leave a message, she immediately asked him to wait and Louella came on.

"Gus? Thanks for calling. You've seen the paper? About Caroline?"

"Yes. I knew her as well, incidentally. Nice lady. I didn't realise she was a friend of yours."

"I first met her in the Sixties and we became very close, probably the nearest thing I had to a sister." Louella sobbed abruptly. "Christ, I daren't cry. I've got a customer to attend to."

"I'm sure they'll understand if you tell them . . . and why are you letting me know about this? Did Caroline ever say she knew me?"

"No, that's not the point." Louella sniffed. "The thing is that she was one of the guests at Barry Kershaw's last party."

"You're throwing me here," Maltravers said. "What are you trying to say? Are you suggesting there's some connection?"

"I'm not sure, but . . . I keep telling myself I'm being stupid, but was it really an accident?"

"The police seem to think so," he replied. "Why shouldn't it be?"

"I don't *know*! It's just that Barry's been in my mind a lot since we talked and . . . God, I'm beginning to sound neurotic. I just don't like it. It . . . worries me. Am I making any sort of sense?"

"Frankly, not much," Maltravers told her. "But why not come round and have supper so we can talk about it?"

"Do you think there is something to talk about?"

"I think that you think there is. That's enough."

Louella sighed gratefully. "If I can just . . . get it out of my system with someone, perhaps I'll be all right. Are you sure you don't mind?"

"Of course not," he assured her. "We're at fourteen Coppersmith Street just off Liverpool Road. We'll expect you here about seven. If you're coming by car, you'll have no trouble parking at that time."

"Thank you. I'll see you then."

She rang off and Maltravers went back into the kitchen where

Tess had finished the potatoes and was preparing a Waldorf salad. "Make extra. I've asked Louella round for supper."

"What's the problem?"

"I'm not sure. It seems that Caroline Owen was at Barry Kershaw's famous party and she's getting in a state about it."

Tess glanced at him sharply. "What's she suggesting?"

"She wasn't specific, but presumably she thinks there could be a connection with Caroline's death."

"After twenty-odd years? Come on. It's just a coincidence."

"Perhaps that's what she needs someone to tell her. Anyway, you've known her for some time. Is she the over-imaginative type? I didn't get that impression."

"You're right," Tess acknowledged. "It's completely out of character for her to start getting hysterical . . . Incidentally, did you mention Barry Kershaw to Jenni Hilton?"

"I casually threw his name at her, and she ducked." Maltravers helped himself to a piece of celery off the chopping board. "I still haven't acquired a taste for walnuts, share mine between yourself and Louella. In fact, she instantly lied, because she said she didn't remember him, which is ridiculous. I let it pass, but it's interesting."

Tess dropped a handful of diced apple into the bowl and continued mixing the salad. "What are you going to do about it?"

"I'm not sure," he said. "Perhaps play at being a crime reporter and see if anything turns up. Whatever's on Louella's mind about Caroline, she's certainly convinced that Kershaw was murdered and . . ." He broke off as the telephone rang. "I'll get it. It might be Mike asking how I got on with the interview."

It wasn't; it was a police sergeant who wanted to ask him about the death of Caroline Owen.

"How did you get on to me?" Maltravers asked.

"Just a routine check, Mr Maltravers. We're contacting everyone who's listed in Mrs Owen's personal address book to see if they can tell us anything."

"Like what?"

"Had she been depressed or worried about anything lately?"

"You mean was she suicidal? I can't help you there. I haven't seen her for . . . I'm not sure . . . about a year. As far as I'm aware, her business was doing all right and I know nothing about her private life."

"Do you know her husband?"

"I knew she was married, but all I know about him is what I've read in the *Standard*. I'm a writer, she used to work for my publisher. That's about it. Sorry."

"That's all right, Mr Maltravers. We have to check these things out."

"Of course." Maltravers hesitated. "The *Standard* says you're treating her death as an accident. Is that right?"

"At the moment we are. Do you know of anything that might make us think differently?"

"No. As I said, I haven't seen her for some time."

"Well, if anything occurs to you, perhaps you'll call me." The sergeant gave his name and the station telephone number. "Sorry to have troubled you. Thank you for your assistance."

Maltravers rang off and rationalised his reaction to the unexpected call. On reflection, the police contacting anyone who knew Caroline Owen seemed obvious once it had happened. Suicide was an option and they had to ask people who knew her how likely it was. If they were working through the address book in alphabetical order, they would soon reach Louella Sinclair's name. He wondered what she would tell them. She was convinced that Barry Kershaw had been murdered; was she now thinking the same about Caroline Owen?

Chapter Six

Maureen Kershaw had stopped grieving and begun to hate the moment she had watched the purple velvet crematorium curtains close on her son's coffin. Fed by obsession, that hatred had first, perversely, comforted her and later become a touchstone to which she could always return. As the years passed, outwardly it seemed she had forgotten, but she would frequently sit alone, smoking and sipping her tea, finding again a purpose to live by drawing on its malevolent energy.

She had been born into and become inescapably part of the values and lifestyle of a pre-war Docklands terrace sliding into a slum, penny-pinching, groceries on tick, petty theft, cheap furniture on the never-never, the tacky glamour of Southend or egg flip in noisy saloon bars of grimy corner pubs. Barry had escaped and entered a foreign world "up West", neon lights, flats of unimaginable luxury, people who wore suits on weekdays—people who *had* suits—smart bars and the dazzle of show business. But she had still been his Mum, fierce with pride when he had arrived in his white Jaguar and dirty nets had twitched jealously at every window in Etruria Street; the tearaway who had first been put on probation when he was ten years old, the son they said would end up in Borstal or worse was sticking two triumphant fingers up at them.

And however rich he had become, however many stars he had met, he had still been her Barry. Flowers, presents, money, love. He had kept wanting to buy her a bungalow in Essex, send her on a world cruise, put young Terry through a posh school, but had accepted that she was content with the only life she had known. Just once she had been persuaded to enter his world. The warm, sleek limousine had picked her up and taken her to some theatre—the name had long gone—where she had stepped nervously out into a glare of lights and an excited crowd on the pavement. Barry had led her up the steps and through the entrance then left her with one of his girls and after that it had all whirled around her until she began to feel sick with helplessness. The girl had said something about the new show being brilliant and kept pointing out famous and beautiful people as the flashlights had exploded, but hardly anyone else had spoken to her. She had known that her dress, chosen with agonising uncertainty out of a mail order catalogue, which had brought cries of approval from her neighbours, was like cheap paste in the company of diamonds. Long before she had escaped back into the safe, anonymous darkness of the limousine for the journey home, she had known she did not belong and swore never to try again.

And after that it had been all right. Barry had still called from time to time, quietly leaving an envelope of money—never too much—where she would find it after he had gone, kicking a football with Terry and the other kids out on the street, throwing off the cloak of his other life and joking with old Mrs Wilson from next door as if he had never been away. And Maureen Kershaw had been happy, living where the sun of his success warmed her but did not scorch.

Then Barry had died and she had become the female animal, too late to save her young's life, but spitting and clawing to protect his name. And the police had sneered about him, and some coroner had stopped her protests and the smoothly dressed filth who said they had known him had lied and lied and lied. They had made out that her shining boy had become like them, corrupted by money and sick for drugs. Nobody had believed her, pretending that she of all people in the world had not really known him. For a long time she had fought, for a long time she had cried, but finally she had retreated into a dark cave of bitterness, clutching her younger son to her, comforting him with her own rage and passing that anger on to him. Because Maureen Kershaw knew who had killed Barry and one day Terry would kill her, however many years it might take.

And now Terry was successful, owing it to no one but himself, just like Barry had been. Together they had left Etruria

Street and its intolerable memories, moving first to the better end of Romford and then out to the house in Brentwood. After Terry had married, he and Stephanie had bought a house near her parents in Highgate, lovely but too small for Maureen to live with them, particularly now the twins were nearly twelve. And Stephanie could be . . . Well, that didn't matter. Every week Terry came to see her, even occasionally staying overnight. Old friends—scattered by the yuppie revolution which had destroyed the East End—visited from time to time, but otherwise Maureen Kershaw lived alone, a life given meaning beyond mere existence by a dream of vengeance. Only a dream until the woman they hated had come back; now a dream that Terry would realise. For Barry.

"I've had more time to think, and perhaps I'm going mad." Louella looked from Tess to Maltravers apologetically. "But I don't like it."

"Obviously." Maltravers handed her a glass of wine. "I knew Caroline—not as well as you—and I don't like the thought of her being dead. But your not liking is heavier than mine. Why?"

"Because it's . . ." Louella shook herself in irritation, ". . . because it's come at a bad time. Just after you were asking me about Barry."

"And you can't just accept coincidence?" asked Tess.

"I know that's common sense," Louella admitted. "But from the moment I read that story in the *Standard*, I've not been able to shake off this weird feeling."

"Based on nothing more than the fact that she was one of the guests at a party umpty-um years ago," Maltravers pointed out. "A bit thin."

"Transparent." Louella looked directly at him. "So tell me I'm neurotic and I'll shut up."

"Not neurotic," he corrected. "But you're upset and perhaps not thinking as straight as usual. Let's talk it through. First of all, what was Caroline's connection with Kershaw? How did they know each other? She never told me much about her past."

"Caroline was a secretary with a record publisher in those days," Louella explained. "Several of Barry's clients were on the label, including Jack's Spratts and Tony Morocco. She was very pretty and out to enjoy herself. All of a sudden, a woman could sow her wild oats like a man without being classed as a tart and Caroline sowed a lot. There were plenty of us like that, making London swing before respectability and middle age got to us."

"So the connection was the record label," Maltravers said. "Anything more to it?"

"Nothing I know of, and Caroline and I had few secrets from each other. She certainly never slept with him or anything."

"But did she give evidence at his inquest?"

"Yes—and that's what's getting to me. She admitted that she didn't know whether or not Barry used LSD or anything else, but was quite prepared to go along with it at the inquest."

"Who for?" Maltravers asked sharply. "Who was she protecting?"

"She didn't know and she didn't care," Louella replied positively. "She said she was just grateful the bastard was dead and after a while we stopped talking about it. It was . . . I don't know . . . an extreme example of something out of line which you do when you're young and stupid and don't think about later."

"Very extreme," Maltravers commented. "But she wasn't the only one and we've been through that. Let's look at it now. Caroline's dead and the police seem to think it was an accident. You think it was something worse . . . So you think that somebody killed her and the reason goes back to Barry Kershaw? Right?"

"That's what I *think*," Louella acknowledged. "But does it make sense?"

"Not much, and you know it. Even if somebody had suspected Caroline had been involved in killing Barry Kershaw, why wait this long before doing something about it?" Maltravers shook his head dismissively. "No way. What about other alternatives? The police rang me earlier—they're working through Caroline's address book—and asked if she might have been suicidal. I couldn't help them, but have they called you yet?"

"They may have rung me at home, but I came straight here from the shop," Louella replied. "Anyway, they can put that right out of their minds. I was with Caroline a couple of weeks ago and she was as suicidal as you are. There must be others who'll confirm that."

"Then let's try another option. Could anyone else have wanted to kill her? The police asked me about her husband, but I don't know anything there apart from the fact they were separated. When did that happen?"

"Ted and Caroline split up about . . . what must it be? . . . a couple of years ago. They'd been married for nearly fifteen years."

"Messy split up?" Maltravers asked.

"No, perfectly civilised. There were no children—Ted couldn't give her any—and the marriage had just withered. Caroline launched Scimitar Press and Owen Graham Metcalf kept Ted over-occupied. Their careers got in the way of their relationship. It happens."

"Incidentally, OGM is the agency behind a television commercial I've just done," Tess said. "In fact, I met Ted Owen. About fifty, very tall, with a little ponytail. Looks like Paul Newman if you get him at the right angle and use your imagination."

"I didn't know about the ponytail, but that's typical of Ted. Always likes to be up with the fashion. Did you meet his girlfriend?"

"Not that I remember."

"Daphne something . . . Daphne Gillie. Less than half his age and, according to Caroline, a right little raver."

"So did she break the marriage up?" Maltravers asked.

Louella shook her head. "No, you can't blame her for that. She joined OGM after the separation. Caroline suspected Ted had been putting it about a bit—his brains are sometimes between his legs, which isn't uncommon—but Daphne arrived later. They're living together now."

"And does Ted Owen go back to the Kershaw days?"

"Not to my knowledge. He was at Cambridge in the Sixties and Caroline met him not long before they married. I never got to know him all that well. After Caroline married we just kept seeing each other the way we always had. It was part of her life that had nothing to do with Ted."

"So the break up was amicable and then a new girlfriend arrived," Maltravers observed. "Happens all the time."

"There was one thing," Louella added. "Ted wants to marry Daphne, but Caroline had dug her heels in over a divorce."

"Why?"

"She was a Catholic. Ted suggested a quickie divorce on the grounds of two years' separation, but Caroline refused because it would mean her agreeing and she couldn't do that. She pointed out that after five years he would be able to divorce her whether she agreed or not. Caroline accepted the marriage was over and that eventually they would divorce. It just had to be on terms where she wasn't an active party to it. Her conscience wouldn't let her."

"And Ted went along with that?" Maltravers queried.

"Eventually, but he pressed pretty hard. Caroline came to see me one night after they'd had a row about it. She said he couldn't seem to grasp there was no panic about marrying Daphne."

"Did he ever stop pressing?"

"I don't know, but I assume he must have done," Louella replied. "He had no choice. Apart from that one night, Caroline hardly spoke about it, so I don't know why he pushed her in the first place."

Maltravers pulled a face as he thought round the situation. "Perhaps he wants to make an honest woman out of Daphne, which would be a novel approach these days. Her father isn't a Victorian hangover threatening to cut her off without a penny for living in sin is he?"

"Her parents are dead," Louella told him. "Caroline heard that from Ted. They were killed in a car crash when she was about fifteen. I can't remember the details, but I think she lived with some relatives in Dorset before she went to university, then moved to London."

"Then I can't see any urgency in making her the next Mrs Owen," Maltravers said. "Pity. If I could, there might be a reason for Ted wanting her dead."

Louella smiled slightly. "Before Ted Owen does anything, he asks two questions. What's the risk factor and what's in it for me? If there's enough in it, he'll take the risk. But murdering

Caroline? Just because she wouldn't give him a divorce? No way."

"It wasn't a serious suggestion," Maltravers acknowledged. "But while we're kicking ideas around, how about someone else? Jilted boyfriend perhaps . . . or a jealous wife?"

"Nothing like that," Louella told him. "Caroline did her share of fooling around a long time ago and was too intelligent to start again. She had Scimitar Press, a bit of charity work through the Church and her friends. She'd got to the stage where she'd rather go to bed with a good book."

"Then face it, Louella," Maltravers said. "You can't come up with anyone who might have wanted to kill her, and if I hadn't seen you by chance and talked about Barry Kershaw just before she died would you be thinking the way you are?"

Louella sighed in acceptance. "Probably not. Thanks for letting me talk it out. It's just that we'd known each other so long and she was such a lovely . . ." She blinked and turned away as her voice stumbled. Tess stood up and put a comforting arm round her shoulders.

"Hey, this isn't like you. Where's that lady who scares the pants off everyone who walks into Syllabub?"

"Did the act fool you as well?" Louella sounded surprised. "It's a professional gimmick and they love it." Reddened eyes were raised to Tess. "But it's not real. This is me without my mask. I cry over any bloody thing."

"I never guessed," Tess told her. "Come on. Sob it out. Supper's ready whenever you want it."

Maltravers went into the front room, partly to leave them alone for a few minutes, partly because he felt uncomfortable over the degree to which Louella's distress was reaching him. His relationship with Caroline Owen had been deeper into friendship than he had realised and affected him more than he expected. Could Louella really be right in thinking there was something wrong about her death? She had no evidence, no reason to be suspicious. He had been talking to her about Barry Kershaw shortly before, but surely that was just coincidence and . . . On the desk was his tape recorder, ready to play back the Jenni Hilton interview. She had lied about not remembering Barry Kershaw for reasons he could only guess at. What secrets were hidden behind lies that went back more than twenty years? How much had Caroline been involved? She certainly hadn't committed suicide, so . . . Had it really been an accident? Because if not . . .

"You've got me thinking," he said as they sat down to supper. "When I mentioned Barry Kershaw to Jenni Hilton this afternoon, she immediately said she couldn't remember him. Reaction?"

Louella looked across the table in amazement. "She couldn't *remember*? That's . . . it's ridiculous. No, more than that. It's stupid. She may as well say she can't remember her own name. Did you press her on it?"

"No—and for the very reason that it was stupid. I wanted to think about it."

"And what have you come up with?"

"Nothing so far, except that she's almost certainly worked out that I knew she was lying. I'm not sure how far I can go in that area, but now that Caroline's dead . . ." He shrugged uncertainly.

"You told me I was being irrational," Louella reminded him.

"It must be catching. Let's say that it wouldn't hurt to try and find out more about it. I've got to deliver my piece on Jenni Hilton to *The Chronicle* in a few days. I'll dig out their crime reporter and see if he can give me any off-the-record stuff on what the police think about Caroline's death."

"You think there could be something then?"

"I don't know, but if there is we'll talk about it again. Caroline and I weren't close friends, but we were always happy to see each other. I don't like to think that somebody might have killed her. There's precious little to suggest that happened, but Jenni Hilton lied to me about Barry Kershaw and until I know why I'll keep my options open."

"Thank you." Louella smiled at him. "It helps when someone doesn't just write me off as mad. How is Jenni, by the way? Apart from her memory."

"Very well, and great fun to talk to."

"You must tell Louella the story of your youth," Tess said slightly caustically. "She actually knew Jenni Hilton when all you had were fantasies."

Maltravers laughed as Louella looked puzzled. "This is embarrassing, but OK. When I was about seventeen . . ."

When Russell had rung from Exeter, she had only been on the first whisky and ginger and it had been all right; she had even joked about trying to recapture the taste of the Sixties again in the drink. He'd found a new flat which he was sharing with three other students, he'd met a girl called Vanessa ("You'll like her. I'll bring her up in the summer vac"). Yes, Dad had written and he was fine, and no, he didn't need anything; stop fussing for Christ's sake. A piece in *The Chronicle*? When? No, of course it wouldn't embarrass him. Sorry, darling, but most of my friends here have never heard of you. Yes, I am working. You're getting boring, Mum, you're becoming middle-aged and conventional. You'll be showing people your holiday slides next. Look, I've got to go. Vanessa is taking me to some pub where they have great jazz. What's that? I've been being careful for years, stupid. Love you.

Now she was on the fourth drink, a mistake because it had started to make her depressed, confusing her thoughts. Russell had gone away and she was back on her own again. Returning to London had not worked; she was yesterday in a city that only knew today. Old friends were delighted to see her, but had only nostalgic fragments of the past to offer. She couldn't imagine doing a Dusty Springfield and recording with the Pet Shop Boys; a vague suggestion that she might like to play Mrs Darling in this year's production of *Peter Pan* had made her feel almost senile. Thinking about a comeback was insane. She should have returned to San Francisco, to Vernon who still wrote his hopeful letters . . . No, it was none of that. It was the needling, constant worry of Augustus Maltravers and his mention of Barry Kershaw. What had he found out? If he referred to it in his piece for *The Chronicle*, how could she persuade him to drop it without making him even more suspicious? Because she knew he was suspicious, however cleverly he had immediately pretended to lose interest when she had said she could not remember. That was sick. Of all the things that had happened in her life, Barry Kershaw and his death was more vivid than the whole whirling kaleidoscope of fame, glamour and excitement. Forget Barry? It would be wonderful if she could.

Chapter Seven

It is a fact of life that everybody dies; it is a fiction that the police immediately start suspecting the worst when they are presented with a corpse. Murder is a relatively rare crime in Britain and is only considered if some unusual factor suggests it. Caroline Owen's death was one of between ninety and a hundred which occur on London's Underground every year and the most likely explanations were natural causes, suicide or accident. A body punctured with stab wounds is obviously a CID matter; otherwise it is probably the result of something non-criminal.

Natural causes—a massive heart attack which killed her even before she went under the train—were ruled out by the pathologist's report which found she was in very good health. There were no drugs in her body, unexplained wounds or anything else suspicious. Even before Caroline Owen's friends had insisted it was unthinkable, the police had thought suicide—almost invariably the reason behind such deaths—was unlikely. People who take their own lives by throwing themselves under Tube trains tend to choose times when stations are quiet and stand next to the entrance tunnel to take advantage of maximum speed; the middle of a platform crowded with rush-hour travellers was all wrong.

Which would have left accident with a clear field, but for one small point that a detective inspector noticed. Ted Owen had told the police there had been no real disagreement between him and his wife over her refusal to co-operate in divorce proceedings. But two of her friends insisted she had been upset about it and, while she had not gone into details, had left them with the impression there had been a major row. Feeling he was doing no more than going through the motions, the inspector checked through the papers for the incident.

Having examined the contents of Caroline Owen's handbag, the police had first gone to Scimitar Press's offices in Covent Garden, but they had been closed. They then visited her flat in Holland Park, talked to the neighbours and let themselves in with her keys. Her personal address book led them to Owen Graham Metcalf where someone working late said Ted Owen had left about seven o'clock to join his girlfriend at the Groucho. Staff at the club confirmed he had been there, but had left with Daphne Gillie to have dinner, destination unknown. The police had taken his home address from the club's membership list and ended up outside a seven hundred and fifty thousand pound Georgian house in Richmond, waiting for him to return.

The inspector swiftly ran through Owen's statement. Separation amicable . . . Not seen wife for about six weeks . . . Still on good terms . . . No financial hassle about the house they had lived in together . . . Gave names of friends who would have seen her more recently than he had . . . Here it was. Discussed a divorce about three months ago on the grounds of two years' separation, but that would need Caroline's agreement. She had refused, he had accepted. In reply to a specific question, said it had been no problem. Pointed out that after another three years, he would be able to arrange a divorce without his wife's consent and he and Daphne Gillie were prepared to wait another three years before they married. Why not?

But . . . the inspector sorted out two other statements—one from Louella Sinclair, the second from another woman—and they insisted she had been angry that he had pressed her so hard. Not much, probably nothing, but worth looking into. It would certainly do no harm to find out where Ted Owen and Daphne Gillie were when Caroline Owen died on the Central Line.

Behind heavy black glass doors, Owen Graham Metcalf's foyer was thick with taste and the invisible aura of money to express it. Successful advertising campaigns which had persuaded the public to buy products ranging from instant frozen meals to exclusive cars, chocolates to sanitary towels, life assurance to beauty creams that owed nothing to animal suffering, had been translated into pale grey and pink décor, luxurious crimson leather chairs, hidden lighting, muted music and a front-of-house receptionist lifted intact off a *Harpers & Queen* cover. Sergeant John Doyle, accustomed both professionally and privately to life at the end of an operation manipulated by copywriters, creative directors, artists and producers of television commercials, reflected that snappy slogans and hummable jingles paid better than he had imagined. The endless washed-strawberry carpet into which his shoes sank as he walked in must have cost about a year's salary in the CID.

Welcoming smile switched on the moment he appeared through the door, the girl behind the desk gave the impression that he was suddenly the most important person in her life. An appointment with Mr Owen? What name, please? And from which company? Oh . . . *Sergeant* Doyle. I see. If you'd like to take a seat, I'll let him know you're here. Thank you. As he sat down, Doyle could almost feel himself plummet in her estimation from a possible major client to a tiresome policeman, the sort who put wheel clamps on Porsches outside wine bars. He was kept waiting a perfectly judged few minutes before a Madonna wannabee took him through to Ted Owen's office, based on an idea by the designers of first-class cabins of the original *Queen Elizabeth*, with the immediate signs of a man surrounded by comprehensive support systems; matt finish ebony desktop bore a white telephone with a hands-free facility, a large diary with a company logo embossed in gold leaf on its cover and a virgin green blotter, but not a single piece of paper. Silver walls were covered with advertising awards framed in brushed aluminium and signed photographs of show business stars who had promoted products for OGM clients. Doyle noted the tasteful black Pierre Cardin tie and look of helpful concern.

"Good-morning, sergeant." Owen did not stand up as he smiled and indicated a leather and tubular-steel chair. "Please sit down. I don't know how I can help you further than I did in my statement, but if there's anything at all . . ." The sentence floated.

"You'll appreciate we have to check everything, sir," Doyle replied and received a graceful nod of acceptance. "It's about your divorce. You said you and your wife did not have an argument over her refusal."

"That's correct." Owen's voice was as blank as his face.

"But other people have told us she was very upset because you pressed her for it."

"I can't be responsible for what other people say," Owen commented. "What other people say my wife said in fact. We discussed it a couple of times, perhaps three, certainly no more. We ended up agreeing to disagree in a perfectly civilised manner. That's all there was to it. This was all in my statement."

"Yes, sir." Doyle paused. "Where were you at the time of your wife's death?"

"Why do you ask?" The chill in the atmosphere was fractional, but instantly there.

"I'd just like to know, sir."

"You're suggesting that I killed her."

"I'm suggesting nothing. I'm just asking where you were."

"Very well." Owen sounded like a man agreeing to be honest with a tax inspector. "You have a job to do, and frankly I thought this might be raised. From about five o'clock until shortly after seven I was in the conference room along the corridor with two of my colleagues and three representatives of a major bank. We were pitching for—sorry, that's jargon—we were showing them the artwork for an advertising campaign with which we hope to win their advertising account. To save tedious questions and answers, sergeant, none of us left the room at any time."

He looked at Doyle levelly. "The fact that these offices are only a few minutes' walk from Tottenham Court Road station is academic. I was here. I can give you the names of the people who were with me if you wish to confirm that. Of course I didn't kill my wife . . . and I happen to be able to prove it."

Doyle was about to ask another question when Owen anticipated him.

"And the next thing you're going to ask is about Miss Gillie, isn't it? The lady I'm now living with. I'll get her in here." He picked up the telephone and rapidly punched three buttons. "Daphne? Sergeant Doyle from the CID is with me. Can you come through, please?"

Replacing the receiver, Owen folded his hands together beneath his chin. For a moment they looked at each other in silence then Owen spoke again. "It was quite obvious to both of us how you were going to think and we've talked about it. However, we're not about to produce another conveniently perfect . . . Well, here she is. She can tell you herself."

Doyle turned as the door opened and a brunette looking younger than he had expected came in. The outfit was power dressing, stiletto heels, black tights, close-fitting Joseph charcoal-grey suit setting off heavy gold necklace and bangle. The face would have been startlingly pretty when it smiled, but was now businesslike and severe, grey-green eyes serious, thin lips set in a straight line of deep scarlet.

"Sergeant Doyle wants to know where you were when Caroline died," Owen said. "I could have explained, but it's better that you tell it."

Daphne Gillie showed no reaction as she sat in the chair next to Doyle. He wondered whether what he was going to hear had been rehearsed or simply made ready in advance to save time.

"I understand the critical time is about twenty to six." She looked straight at him as he spoke. "I wish I could say exactly where I was, but I can't. I left here about five fifteen, did some window shopping on Oxford Street, then went to the Groucho where Ted was going to meet me when he'd finished his meeting."

"What time did you arrive at the club?" Doyle asked.

"I wish I knew." Daphne Gillie emphasised her answer slightly. "Possibly somebody I met there or one of the girls on the desk might remember, but all I can say is that it was about six o'clock."

"Which means, of course, that she was in the area of Tottenham Court Road station at the wrong time," Owen put in. "Let's get on with it, sergeant, we're all busy people. It's cards on the table time. Daphne did not murder my wife, but has no way of proving it. We can let you have a photograph to take round some of the shops she wandered in and out of and perhaps an assistant will remember seeing her and will be able to say what time it was. Somebody at the Groucho may be able to help. I don't know. But I do know two things."

He leaned forward, elbows on the desk and touched one forefinger against the other. "One. If Daphne and I had planned to kill my wife, then obviously we would have made bloody sure that each of us had an alibi. I have one, but only by chance. Daphne doesn't, which suggests we're either rather stupid or simply innocent." The forefinger moved. "Two. Why should we want to kill Caroline? There was no animosity between her and me, and don't let the fact that I'm back at work so soon start you thinking that I'm not distressed at her death. We may have separated, but we were very happily married for a number of years. I regret her death and had no reason either to wish it or bring it about—and neither did Daphne."

"I'd like to say something else," Daphne Gillie put in. "Until Ted talked to me about it, I never thought for one moment that either of us could be suspected. When he persuaded me it was possible, I began to think of anything that could prove I'm innocent. But I didn't spend the evening carefully making sure there were witnesses who would be able to account for my movements in case the police asked me about them later. People don't live their lives like that."

"Did you know Mrs Owen?" Doyle asked her.

"We'd never met, although Ted pointed her out to me in St Martin's Lane when we were out one evening. I don't think she saw us. She was with someone."

Doyle hesitated. The inspector who had sent him had admitted it was a long shot and the police had no reason to start pushing it. As he paused, Owen opened a drawer in his desk.

"A photograph of Daphne." He thrust it across the desk with a page from an OGM memo pad. "Perhaps you'll find someone who'll remember her. She's written down what shops she can remember going into."

"Thank you." Doyle picked up the photograph. "You seem to have anticipated everything, sir."

Owen shrugged. "Common sense, sergeant. Nothing suspicious. Looking at all the options is part of my job—even the unlikely ones. Is there anything else?"

There wasn't and Doyle was taken back to reception. Owen and Daphne Gillie stood at the window, watching him consult the list of shops before walking away towards Oxford Street.

"PC Plod's off to check your story," he remarked. "Wouldn't it be nice if someone came up with something?"

"Don't count on it," she said. "There's as much chance of that as of someone coming up with a motive."

Doyle reported back to the station two hours later. One assistant had vaguely recognised the picture, but could not say if Daphne Gillie had been in the shop at any time on the evening Caroline Owen died. The girls at the Groucho remembered her arriving . . . sometime after five thirty? Members signed the book at reception, but did not put the time. When did Frank Muir arrive? It was after that. Or was it before? Perhaps six o'clock? Or . . . sorry. The inspector was philosophical.

"I'd have been a sight more suspicious if they'd both had cast-iron alibis," he remarked. "Owen's not the type to commit murder unless he had one hell of a reason and there's damn all that I can see. Let the coroner sort it out."

Which the coroner subsequently did. He heard evidence that Caroline Owen was not suicidal and that police inquiries had produced nothing suspicious. It had all the hallmarks of an accident, but nobody had come forward, guiltily confessing they must have pushed too hard on the crowded platform in their anxiety to get on the train. It lay on the file as an open verdict and the police lost interest. Murder? Forget it. That sort of thinking was for fiction.

Vincent Mulchrone, one of the most gifted writers ever to adorn the columns of the *Daily Mail*, once remarked that journalism must be the only human endeavour where the orgasm comes at the beginning. Constantly rewording the first paragraph of his interview, Maltravers struggled for more than half an hour before he was satisfied with his intro, the critical hook with which to catch the readers' attention.

Mop-headed and ridiculously young, the Beatles grin out of a silver-framed photograph on the mantelpiece, the message "We love you, Jenni, yeah, yeah, yeah!" scrawled by John Lennon above the four signatures. There are no other indications in the room that the beautiful 44-year-old woman with a son at Exeter University was once a pop singer, actress and star. When I comment on the picture, Jenni Hilton smiles ruefully. "It reminds me how old I am. Ringo's a grandfather now for God's sake."

After that it flowed and an instinct born of years in journalism ended it within fifty words of the required two thousand.

Why did she disappear and give up so much? However discreetly the question is asked, the barriers come down, the seal of privacy is carefully protected. Part of Jenni Hilton was never public property and never will be. The moves towards a comeback are cautious and will be on her terms.

The last paragraph was rewritten as often as the first before Maltravers let it go. It was as near as he could get to capturing her but, as he read through the piece, he was aware of the moments when he had failed to bypass the act, when Jenni Hilton had taken control of the interview and deflected him. It had been a game which both had known they were playing and each had silently acknowledged the other's victories. But at lunch, when her defences had been down and he had unexpectedly thrown Barry Kershaw at her, she had been unprepared and responded with a clumsy lie. So now he had baited the piece with a brief mention of Kershaw—nothing contentious, just the indisputable facts of his death and her presence at the inquest. Mike Fraser had assured him she would only be able to correct what she could prove were errors of fact; Maltravers felt convinced she would object to any mention of Kershaw. If she did want it removing, he could ask for a reason, but did not expect to be given one. That was academic, anyway. The mere fact that she asked would show that what happened more than twenty years ago still mattered to Jenni Hilton in some way. And she had not forgotten it.

Chapter Eight

Haphazard genetic chance had given Terry Kershaw a level of intelligence alien to that of his family. Barry had been street-smart, matching his mother's shrewd cunning. Their father could calculate the combination of darts to achieve any given score faster than a computer, but it was an idiot savant ability; otherwise, he could barely spell his own name. A cuckoo in a nest of sparrows, Terry had found his difference disorientating and it had been exaggerated by the influence of a schoolteacher, who, recognising unexpected potential, had opened his mind to codes of behaviour different to those of his home. Then, when he was fifteen and becoming aware of an inexpressible dissatisfaction, Barry had died and his mother had begun to suffocate him, first with her grief, then with her anger, finally with her constant insistence that somehow he owed it to her to avenge Barry. The teacher left his school around the same time and Terry lost a critical counterbalancing compensation as Maureen Kershaw relentlessly manipulated his confused loyalty. He was all she had left. She would never stand in his way and he must be successful like Barry had been, but there had been endless twists of emotional blackmail, confusing and caging him.

For ten years he and Maureen had lived together, her bitterness over Barry's death coagulating into a resentment that dominated her life. Terry's realisation that he had not particularly liked his brother had driven him into a turmoil of private guilt at what his conditioned conscience told him was a betrayal of the love he ought to feel for his mother. By his mid-twenties, he had come to terms with it by splitting his personality. At home with Maureen he was still the East End son, supportive and faithful; in town, as he built up his car retail business, he created another life more subtle and sophisticated, into which he could escape. Night-school classes which he explained away as a business course were actually elocution lessons to teach him to speak the language of his alternative existence. That deception produced the unbreachable split in him; he found he was unable to belong wholly in two worlds and had to choose one for reality and one for pretence. From then on, Maureen Kershaw only received the act, although he continued to make it appear the truth.

He met Stephanie when her father's company bought out his four profitable showrooms. The initial negotiations took place in Bernard Driffield's home, and it was a measure of the distance Terry Kershaw had travelled that he was more comfortable in The Bishop's Avenue, Hampstead than in Etruria Street, Wapping. Driffield remarked to his wife and daughter afterwards how impressed he was that a man in his twenties could have built up his own business so successfully and the proposed buyout would add a valuable new member to the board of Insignia Motors. Three months and a quarter of a million pounds later, Terry Kershaw became national sales director. Intrigued by someone who had reached her level from nothing, Stephanie Driffield began to include him in her social life and eventually coolly decided she would marry him. Being the chairman's daughter gave her everything her sense of snobbery wanted; being the wife of the man who would almost certainly be her father's successor offered the reassurance that the situation would continue. Flattered by her attention and captivated by blonde, sensual beauty, Terry Kershaw never perceived her real motives and by the time he realised she was a bitch it was too late. From then on he was torn between two powerful women.

Stephanie and Maureen Kershaw had recognised each other for what they were the moment they met; mutual contempt, smooth on one side, savage on the other, simmered under a veneer of tolerance. Terry constantly tried and repeatedly failed as a peacemaker throughout several years of battles and finally gave up over the Highgate house. His suggestion that it was big enough for his mother to live with them precipitated a row in which Stephanie ruthlessly used every weapon in her considerable armoury. The uneasy peace that eventually came was based on Maureen's apparent retreat, but she clung on to one part of her son, a defeated general maintaining a guerrilla resistance in the mountains. Every week he visited her—ignoring Stephanie's caustic scorn about "running home to his Mum—and Maureen used the dripfeed of what she believed was their shared private hatred for Barry's killer, still because she wanted revenge, but also because it meant she and Terry had something which kept them together. He never disillusioned her as the litany of hate became increasingly meaningless because he knew it was all she had left. It didn't matter anyway; it was something that would never be activated. Then one morning, Maureen telephoned him at the office.

"Terry!" Her voice was tight with excitement. "She's back in London!"

"Who is, Mum?"

"Jenni Hilton. Who do you think?"

For a moment he was bewildered, then appalled as a sleeping spectre awoke to face him. The day of Barry's funeral when his mother had frightened him, first with the rigid cold of her grief, then with the searing heat of her anger, leapt back to him. Helpless to assuage her, he had been battered by the animal fury which had poured over him. However many years had passed, however much he had pushed it all away, he still carried the scars of that night and suddenly felt the sting of reopened wounds.

"Jenni Hilton?" Mind and emotions were reeling. "How do you know?"

"It's in the *Daily Express*. She was at the theatre last night." He heard her take a triumphant breath of satisfaction. "After all this time."

"Look, someone's with me," he lied hastily. "I'll come and see you this evening." He half lowered the phone, then snatched it back to his mouth. "Just stay in. Don't do anything."

He rang off and stared at a disputed invoice on his desk, figures as incomprehensible as hieroglyphics, before opening a drawer and hastily swallowing two of the pills his doctor had prescribed for stress. Then he went down to reception where all the morning papers were provided for waiting customers. Back in his office, he read the Diary piece in the *Express*, examining Jenni Hilton's face as though she was some fabled malignant creature in whose existence he had never really believed. As the shock of his mother's call began to recede, all the irrationality of her behaviour reached him. Apart from the fact that revenge for Barry after more than twenty years was sick, there was not a shred of evidence that Jenni Hilton had been responsible for his death; Maureen Kershaw had based her conviction on nothing more substantial than the mysterious disappearance, inexplicable to everyone except herself.

"She's run away so she won't get found out," she had hissed when she read the constant reports. "It must have been her in Barry's flat that night who answered the phone when that reporter rang."

His cautious arguments that she could be wrong were dismissed. Why should anyone give up all that success, all that adulation, most importantly all that money, without a reason? She'd been one of the worst liars at Barry's inquest, now she was scared that someone would come out with the truth and had scuttled away to hide. For weeks Maureen Kershaw had scoured newspapers, frustrated at the conflicting reports of where Jenni Hilton might be, and even now—he suddenly saw the depth of an obsession which he had failed or refused to recognise—even now she had every morning paper delivered for the same reason. For a son who had died in 1968.

Terry Kershaw lay the paper down and swivelled round in his executive chair, gazing across the flat roof of the showroom below his window at the traffic flowing along London's North Circular Road. Did any of those drivers also have a wife who only tolerated them and a mother who was mad?

Jenni Hilton removed her reading glasses—a vanity she mocked herself for kept their necessity secret—as she finished Maltravers's account of their meeting. There was so much about it that she liked, his understated skill with words, the apt and telling adjectives, the acute observations. But there was that single, bald paragraph, discreetly inserted towards the end, apparently innocent to the reader but loaded with dangers. She could not believe that he had included the information just because it was there; his casual comment over lunch had revealed something of how his mind was working. How could she persuade him to remove it without making him more suspicious than he probably was already? She read the word-processor type again more carefully, making a couple of marks in the margin, then found the scrap of paper on which he had written his telephone number.

"Gus Maltravers? It's Jenni Hilton. How are you?"

"Fine. Good to hear from you." He picked up a pen and scribbled her name on a pad; he wanted a record of their conversation. "Has *The Chronicle* sent you my copy?"

"Yes, that's what I'm calling about."

"Any problems?" he asked mildly.

"Only a couple of minor things . . ." There was a pause as she put her glasses back on, "I wasn't brought up in Paris. I was born there because my father was stationed at the British Embassy, but we came back to England about a year later. I spent my childhood in Hertfordshire."

"I'll fix that. Anything else?"

"I'd forgotten about my son's birthday. It's tomorrow, which means he'll be nineteen, not eighteen as I told you. Better get it right."

"Of course." Maltravers waited to see if there were going to be any other minor corrections before she reached what he was certain was the real motive for the call. He wrote the shorthand outlines for "change of tone" on the pad when she spoke again.

"And why have you included a paragraph about Barry Kershaw?"

I'm certainly not going to tell you that, he thought, as he parried with his own question. "Is there anything wrong with it? I'm sure I mentioned his name at some point."

"Yes, but that was afterwards . . . at lunch. It never came up in the interview."

"I thought it had," Maltravers lied. "I came across it when I was doing my research."

"That's not what you said," she told him sharply. "You told me that someone who used to know me had mentioned him. Louella . . . something."

"Louella Sinclair. Now I think about it, you're right, but I knew about it before." She tried to say something else, but he deliberately overrode her. "Anyway, is what I've written wrong? Hang on, I've got my own copy here. Near the end isn't it . . . here we are. 'Jenni Hilton's disappearance came a few weeks after she gave evidence at the inquest into the death of Sixties pop promoter Barry Kershaw. There were attempts to link the two events, but there was nothing to show they were connected. Newspaper efforts to turn a coincidence into some sort of scandal owed more to imagination than reality.' That's right isn't it?"

"Yes, but I can't see that it's relevant . . . It isn't relevant. I would like it taken out, please."

She braced herself for an argument. She had accepted *The Chronicle*'s terms that she could only correct any errors of fact, not information or comment which Maltravers chose to include. But the risks of pressing him to leave it out were less dangerous than what people might start to remember if the paragraph was published. She wanted Barry Kershaw's death to remain buried.

"No problem," he agreed unexpectedly. "I'll tell them to drop it."

"Oh." He smiled at the surprise in her voice. "Will they?"

"Why not? A background par from more than twenty years ago isn't that important. Nobody ever established a connection with your disappearance and there's nothing to suggest there was one. I came across it in my research, but if I'd realised it would upset you, I wouldn't have used it in the first place. Don't worry about it."

"Can I believe you?" she asked cautiously.

"Totally," he assured her. "They're planning to run it on Saturday and that par will not be in. Trust me . . . By the way, did you read about Caroline Owen?"

"Pardon?" The switch of conversation threw her momentarily. "Oh, yes. She was killed on the Underground wasn't she? How do you know that I knew her?"

"Louella again. I knew her as well. Was she a close friend of yours?"

"Fairly, but we haven't been in touch for years. It was an accident wasn't it?"

"That's certainly what the police think . . . Anyway, sorry about the Kershaw business, but we've sorted that. I'd still like you to come round for dinner sometime. Tess wants to meet you."

"Fine . . . but I'm going to Exeter on Saturday to see Russell. I'll be back next Wednesday."

"I'll call you after that. Now I'll get on to the office and take that par out. Leave it with me. Cheers."

Tess walked into the room as Maltravers rang off. "Who was that?"

"La belle Hilton." He did not look up as he reread his notes. "I lied to her slightly . . . but I think she lied to me a lot."

"What about?"

"The late and greatly unlamented Kershaw. She lied better than when I mentioned his name when we met, but if that paragraph . . ." he tapped a sheet of his copy, "is so irrelevant, why is she so anxious that it doesn't go in?"

Tess crossed to the desk and read over his shoulder. "Will it go in?"

"No, because I've promised it won't." He smiled cynically. "But I know that it was there . . . and I know that it worried her."

"So is it relevant?" Tess asked.

"It has to be," he replied. "I can't see how—and I certainly can't see any connection with Caroline's death—but I'd like a bit more information."

"Who from?"

"Louella. What time is it? I'll ring her and suggest a pub lunch somewhere." He picked up the telephone again. "But first, a call to *The Chronicle* . . . and not just to tell them to exorcise the ghost of Kershaw."

He called Mike Fraser on his direct line and sorted out the deletion with a spurious explanation that Jenni Hilton had been upset by it, then asked for the name of the paper's crime reporter.

"Matt Hoffman," Fraser told him. "What do you want him for?"

"Bit of off-the-record stuff he might be able to let me have. If it turns out there's a story in it I'll keep him posted. Can you put me through?"

"Sure. Good piece, incidentally. Nothing that one of the subs won't be able to tidy up . . . I assume you're prepared to trust us with your gilded prose?"

"Unlike some writers, I have a great respect for sub-editors," Maltravers replied. "At least the ones who know that the secret of cutting copy is to do it so that it doesn't bleed. A lot of my stuff has been improved by them."

"I'll give it to a freelance who's working for us at the moment," Fraser said. "He's an artist. Hang on and I'll transfer you to Matt."

The line went silent for a moment, then a faintly Boston American voice announced "Home News".

"Matt Hoffman? Hi. My name's Gus Maltravers. Mike Fraser, the features editor, gave me your name. I'm interested in a woman called Caroline Owen who was killed at Tottenham Court Road Tube station a couple of days back. Did you carry anything on it?"

"I think we had a brief. Accident. There was nothing in it."

"There may have been," Maltravers told him. "If there is, it could be a good story. If you can get me some background, I'll chase it from there. Anything I turn up you can have as an exclusive. I'm not in the business of writing news stories any more."

"What sort of background?"

"Just any inquiries the police made after her death . . . particularly about her husband and his girlfriend."

"What's going on?" Hoffman sounded interested.

"I don't know . . . but I think there's something. Can you do it?"

"I can try," Hoffman agreed. "Things are fairly quiet at the moment. Where can I get back to you?" Maltravers gave him the number. "OK, but the deal is that you give me any results."

"Chapter and verse," Maltravers promised. "Thanks."

During the call, Tess had been reading his feature again. "You persuaded Louella to accept that Caroline's death was an accident and nothing to do with Kershaw," she said as he rang off. "Did you mean it?"

"At the time, yes, but now that Jenni Hilton's risen to the bait, I'm becoming intrigued." For a few moments, he stared out of the window, mentally running over what he knew. "Louella is convinced Kershaw was murdered and at least half suspects the same thing happened to Caroline. Jenni Hilton deliberately lied about knowing Kershaw when I first mentioned his name and is worried about anything to do with him appearing in my feature. Only connect."

"How?"

"That's what we need to find out."

Daphne Gillie's eyes were frost hard as she stared down the account executive, nearly twenty years her senior, sitting opposite.

"OGM doesn't carry passengers and I don't take prisoners," she said coldly. "You've screwed up for the last time. Go and find a crap agency where you'll fit in. We'll post your severance pay."

As the man went red with incipient anger, she opened a file and began to look through rough drafts for a new campaign, writing occasional comments with a solid silver propelling pencil; it was as though he had simply ceased to exist.

"I want to see Ted."

"He's busy. I've told you the position."

As she continued indifferently, he remembered when Daphne Gillie had arrived at the agency and had started the manipulation which he—and several other men—had recognised too late. She had been anxious to please and eager to learn, constantly questioning them, replacing her ignorance of the business by absorbing all they knew with frightening assimilation and total recall. There had been occasional flashes of temper towards her own generation, but she had flattered the senior executives, teasing middle-aged men with the possible chance of very personal attentions if that was necessary. By the time her relationship with Ted Owen had emerged from discreet liaison to open affair, she was established and confident enough to let another side reveal itself; ambitious, nail hard and ruthless. Now she was only pleasant to top executives of the most prestigious global agencies in the West End and Madison

Avenue; she no longer needed the people who had helped her and had no intention of helping them in return. A gleam of sunshine through a chance gap between the high office blocks outside broke into glittering fragments as it caught the diamond locked in a circle of rubies on her left hand.

"You couldn't wait could you?" he said. Only a momentary stillness of the moving pencil indicated that she was aware he had spoken. "Caroline Owen's body isn't cold yet and you're already flaunting that ring."

He was not a weak man—such do not survive in the advertising world—but her response devastated him. Instead of an explosion of anger which would at least have given the satisfaction of a final stand-up cat fight, she reacted with the calm of a professional killer clinically pulling the trigger on a helpless victim. Without looking up from what she was doing, she quietly destroyed him.

"Strange, I never thought you were stupid. You're not just finished with OGM now, you're finished full point. I will personally make sure that no agency that's even half good will take you on. I know the people and I can do that. Now, if you're not out of this building within sixty seconds, I will call security and have you thrown out. Your secretary will clear your desk and we'll send on anything that belongs to you."

Her voice had the emotion of a judge passing a death sentence without any ameliorating hope of the mercy of God. He was too shaken to even slam the door as he left. Daphne Gillie calmly completed her comments on the artwork before contacting Ted Owen on the intercom.

"He's gone," she said tersely.

"Any blood on the walls?"

"Only his. When are we meeting his replacement?"

"Lunchtime at Kensington Place. Seventy-five grand and a top-of-the-range BMW will clinch it. Incidentally, I've just fixed the honeymoon. QEII to New York, three weeks in Barbados and home by Concorde. You like?"

Daphne Gillie's feline growl of pleasure was filled with satisfaction and sensual anticipation. "I *like!*"

*

Why had he agreed so quickly? Why hadn't he argued, defended what he had written? What was he plotting? Jenni Hilton ricocheted between reassuring explanations—he really was an honest and ethical journalist—and frightening ones—he had the scent of a story in his nostrils and was tracking it like a hunter. Suppose he had deflected her with a lie and the paragraph actually appeared? She wouldn't be able to do anything about it. It wasn't libellous and if she played hell with him it would only confirm what he was thinking . . . but what *was* he thinking? And why had he mentioned Caroline? The police said it had been an accident. Did he know something that . . .? As she stared blankly at the birthday card she was about to send to Russell, she felt fear creeping through her.

Chapter Nine

Whether from man-made greenhouse gases or natural vagaries that make weather forecasting in England as hazardous as backing horses, it had become stiflingly hot. London's pavements were an anvil beaten by a hammer of scorching sun, smothered by a thick blanket of motionless ozone-polluted haze that blurred vistas of domes and offices. Windows thrown open for relief (air-conditioning is nearly as rare in Britain as centrally-heated igloos), only offered air unbreathably thick in exchange for air unbreathably stale. Several million throbbing exhausts, many snarled up in ovens of traffic jams, added torrid poisonous fumes to a cauldron of panting animals and sweltering human beings. Underground tunnels offered temporary relief, but only before entering a furnace again. City gents still went to work in dark suits and ties because none dared defy sartorial tradition, but all clothing became sticky with dripping sweat. Movement was wading through warm treacle, lying naked outside was an invitation to be baked alive, staying indoors gave a feeling of being trapped by raging forest fire.

"Definitely on the warm side," Maltravers commented as he placed three spritzers containing enough ice to alarm the captain of the *Titanic* on the garden table of the Chiswick pub where he and Tess had arranged to meet Louella Sinclair. Despite having chosen a spot at least half shaded by a copper beech, their wooden seats were painful to sit on and twenty yards away the waters of the Thames oozed like sluggish oil about to ignite.

"Don't even joke about it," Tess groaned. She loathed excessive temperatures. "I'd rather play Joan of Arc with a real ending."

Perspiration was beginning to smudge Louella's make-up as

she looked at Maltravers sitting opposite her. "What's happened?"

"Nothing to get too excited about yet," he warned her. "But enough to make me start wondering."

"About Caroline?"

"Yes." Caution dragged out the word. "But I think it would be better to start with Barry Kershaw. Accepting your conviction that he was murdered, let's start making guesses about who did it . . . or arranged for it to be done."

"I told you, it could have been any one of . . . God knows how many people," Louella told him. "Just hold on to the fact that everybody hated him."

"Murder's a quantum leap beyond hatred," he replied. "If it wasn't, a few news editors I've known would be corpses. It needs a more powerful trigger to actually kill someone than simply wishing they were dead . . . and I have a suggestion about who could have had that trigger. Jack Buxton."

He paused and drank while the suggestion settled. "Obviously, there's no absolute proof that Kershaw arranged for him to be worked over, but it's bloody likely. Buxton knew that better than anyone . . . so did he do something about it?"

"But he wasn't at the party," Louella pointed out.

"I imagine he found it sick being on the same planet as Kershaw, let alone in the same room," Maltravers remarked. "But he could have made other arrangements."

"Who with?"

"There was evidence at the inquest that some unidentified woman was in Kershaw's flat late that night." Eyebrows damp with a sheen of sweat raised slightly. "Accomplice? Come on, don't tell me it hasn't occurred to you."

"Not for a long time, but . . . yes, there was talk about it," Louella admitted. "Nobody came up with a name though. Not for certain."

"For uncertain then?" he queried. "What names were in the frame?"

"Quite a lot, to be honest. Jack was just about as popular as Barry was detested."

"How about Caroline Owen or Jenni Hilton?"

"They were mentioned."

Maltravers irritably waved away the presence of some buzzing creature as it zipped round his face; moving at such speed in such temperatures was obscene.

"Let's concentrate on them, then. How close were either of them to Jack Buxton?"

Louella fished a cube of ice from her glass and sucked it for a moment. "Jack was very attractive. Plenty of girls went for him, but the fact that you went to bed with someone didn't mean much . . . To be honest, I can't actually remember if he laid me. I think he did once. It was like that. Chastity was definitely not fashionable. So it depends what you mean by close. Caroline or Jenni may have slept with Jack, but just for another ride on the merry-go-round." She suddenly grinned. "Where did we get the bloody energy?"

"The summers must have been cooler," Maltravers commented. "But leaving bedrooms out of it, were Caroline or Jenni ever more than that with Jack?"

"Perhaps. Jack was much more intelligent than a lot of the pop stars and often wanted to talk about politics and religion, things that mattered. Caroline and Jenni were like that as well—so was I—so there was more than just a hedonistic link between them. Whether it ever went deeper than that I don't know."

"But it could have done." Maltravers looked at her very directly. "Could Caroline, with or without Jenni's help, have killed Kershaw because Jack asked her to?"

Louella's fingers twisted a thin gold chain at her throat as he faced her with the possibility.

"I don't like to think she could," she replied finally. "But I've got to accept it's possible. I'm certain somebody did it and I can't pick and choose who I'd like it to have been."

"That's brave of you, Louella," Tess said quietly. "Sorry it's too hot to take your hand for comfort."

Louella smiled at her, then turned back to Maltravers. "Do you really suspect that Caroline killed Barry?"

"That's too big a step yet," he replied. "We need to know more about her and Jack Buxton before we can start thinking like that. What happened to him?"

"He quit the business and married . . . what was her name?

. . . Kate Austin. She was a dancer. They stayed in London for a while, then bought a guesthouse at Porlock in Somerset. I stayed with them one night a few years ago. I must have their business card somewhere."

"Dig it out and let me have the address," Maltravers said. "I'll persuade *The Chronicle* that he could be the focus of another back to the Sixties piece and take it from there."

"Darling, he's hardly going to blurt out that he arranged Kershaw's death," Tess objected.

"I'm going to use a rather more subtle approach than 'Good-morning, are you a murderer? Please confess everything into this tape recorder.'" Maltravers looked at Tess with mock concern. "Is this heat addling your brain? I hope not, because I want you to come with me. Don't worry, it'll be cooler in the Quantocks."

Skin like a crumpled manila envelope, Maureen Kershaw's face was rigid with the shock of a believer whose life-giving faith has been shattered. Fingers, twisted as a knot of roots, lay clenched on the dark olive-green of her skirt, white showing on painfully squeezed knuckles. Through the open window of the echoingly silent room, children's laughter came from the next-door garden. She turned to face her son, but he was leaning forward in the chair, hands clasped together, staring down at rich blue patterns on the carpet. He did not raise his head as she spoke with hoarse bitterness.

"You promised. You promised time and time again. It was the only thing I've ever asked you to do for me. Now you won't."

"I've told you. I can't." Terry Kershaw was suddenly conscious that over the previous half-hour his voice had lost its false polish of elocution and he sounded as though he had never left the East End. It was all part of a relationship his mother had thought special and he had known was deceit. "For God's sake, Mum, I'm not a murderer."

"Not for bloody God's sake," she snapped. "For Barry's sake. For your brother. For my sake. Look at me when I'm talking to you!"

Childhood conditioning instantly obeyed the command. All he saw was a stranger who used to be his mother, features which he still could remember as impishly merry when he had been a toddler made cruelly serpentine by cancerous depths of resentment. How mad had she become?

"It's Stephanie, isn't it?" she demanded. "Snotty bitch with her la-di-dah voice. She's got at you again, hasn't she?"

"Christ Almighty." He sighed with weariness. Did she really think he had told Stephanie—or anybody else—about this? "Stephanie knows nothing except that Barry died years ago. We never talk about him." From some churning well of emotion, a shaft of long repressed honesty leapt out. "I get more than enough of him in this fucking house!"

"Wash your mouth out with soap!" The instinctive order was directed at the child she had been able to control, not the man she had lost. He turned away in frustration; there were no channels of communication left. When had the final one crumbled? They had corroded so subtly over a lifetime that it was impossible to tell.

"Anyway, that's how it is." He stood up. "Sorry, Mum, but it's just not on. I'll see you as usual next week."

"Sit down while I think."

He almost refused, but the commanding glitter of beady eyes snatched him back. Maureen Kershaw's pinched nostrils flared as she breathed in and out deeply. "All right. But you can't refuse to do one thing for me. Find out where she lives."

"Why?" The request instantly alarmed him.

"I want to send her a Christmas card," she replied sarcastically.

"Mum, I don't think—"

"You think too bloody much," she interrupted savagely. "Not straight, but too much. Just let me have the address, then forget about it. Run home to Stephanie and she can wipe your backside for you."

"I don't know how to find where she lives," he said evasively.

"Ring the *Express*. They could know."

"They might not tell me."

"Then try somewhere else. Get that private detective who chases bad debts for you on to it. Just find her." Maureen Kershaw drew herself upright, challenging a refusal. "A street and a number. That's all I want. Don't tell me you won't even do that for me, Terry?"

"What will you do if I manage it?"

"Ask no questions, hear no lies." Another echo of the litany of childhood. "But I'll make you a promise. Once you've told me, I'll never mention her to you again. And I keep my promises. Remember that."

He knew that he should refuse, that agreeing was only pandering to a dangerous sickness in her. The adult he had become wanted to say no, rejecting the request and its grotesque motives; but the child he had been made into flinched from cutting the last terrible knots that had bound them together. Finally, he yielded to obedience forged by a distorted, greedy and possessive love.

"All right. I'll find out somehow."

Maureen Kershaw nodded very slightly. She could tell that she had not lost all her territory of him. She would, of course, but not before he had delivered a final offering. Then it would be just her and Barry, closer in death than in life, together in a burning vengeance. Brentwood neighbours who thought they knew the little old woman could never have imagined that she was consumed by depths of hatred that belonged in fictional passion, not in the local supermarket or Thursday chats when she collected her old age pension in the post office.

When Maltravers and Tess returned to Coppersmith Street, there were two messages on the ansaphone. One was Louella giving them Jack Buxton's address and telephone number, the other from Owen Graham Metcalf to say there was to be a launch party at their offices for the washing-up liquid campaign that included Tess's voice.

"They're mad," she said impatiently. "I'm embarrassed enough about it already, without having to parade in front of people who want to talk about it. I'm not going."

"*Au contraire*," Maltravers told her. "You said Ted Owen was around when you recorded the voice-over, so he's almost certain to be at the shindig. And we can assume that the lovely Daphne Gillie will be there as well. It's a perfect opportunity."

"What for?" Tess's tone revealed she was only procrastinating. Her personal disinclination to have anything to do with the event still had to recognise its possibilities.

"You know full well and fine," replied Maltravers, who had caught the tone. "Endless free booze and everybody wanting to party. All we do is stay sober and see what information or indiscretions spill out."

"What sort of indiscretions?"

"I don't know . . . but I'll be very disappointed if we don't come away with something. You flutter your eyelashes at the men and leave the women to me." He grinned mischievously. "I'll wear my Lambourghini aftershave. You know how irresistible I become."

"Don't delude yourself," she told him. "You're too old for a toy-boy and too young for a sugar daddy. Just be grateful for what you've got."

"I am, but leave me my illusions. Anyway, call OGM back full of girlish acceptance and make sure you can take a partner along. When you've finished, I'll ring Mike Fraser and talk him into letting me do a piece on Jack Buxton."

Tess scowled, but picked the phone up and began to punch in the agency's number. "All right, I'll do it for Louella if nothing else . . . How close are you to believing that Caroline was murdered?"

"Some way to go," Maltravers replied. "But I think she could have been. The problem is trying to find the links which join the odd ends together. Caroline and Jenni Hilton both knew Kershaw and Buxton. According to Louella, Ted Owen was at university in the Sixties, but that would only have been for three years—and Cambridge isn't that far from London anyway. There could have been overlaps that Louella doesn't know about. Owen's home could have been in London and he spent the vacs here. Lot of possibilities and . . ."

He stopped as someone at OGM answered the phone and Tess asked to be put through to the girl who had left the message. Maltravers was amused by another of her spontaneous bits of acting that the acceptance required. By the time she rang off, the girl must have been convinced that the invitation was the biggest thing in Tess's life.

"Your capacity to lie so convincingly worries me sometimes," he remarked as he picked up the phone himself to ring *The Chronicle*. "Do you ever do it to me?"

"Constantly. I have dozens of secret lovers and you've never guessed. I'm going for a shower."

"Then tell them to start buying you flowers," he called after her. "It'll save me money . . . Hello? Mike Fraser, features, please."

When Tess came down again, Maltravers was consulting a road atlas. "I'm seeing Jack Buxton on Saturday." He flicked over a page. "I've booked us in to stay the night as well. While I'm doing the interview, you can chat to his wife—Kate, wasn't it?—and see if she knows anything worthwhile."

Pulling a face, he checked the route again. "Dammit, it looks like the M4. Brain death in concrete. Let's hope it's worth it."

Chapter Ten

Stephanie Kershaw let her husband make love to her in the same way that someone would unexpectedly show affection to a beaten dog, confusing his loyalty. She had grown to despise him, but was not going to put her lifestyle at risk through a divorce. As well as liking him, her father respected him as a businessman and was already thinking of becoming executive president of Insignia Motors with his son-in-law as the new chairman. That would keep him occupied at the office even more, leaving her ample time to indulge her private life. Sex was only made tolerable by closing her eyes and imagining she was in bed with either of her two lovers.

Although she never knew it, one of the repeated pinpricks of scorn she thrust into her husband drew dangerous blood. After leaving the suffocating presence of his mother, Terry Kershaw had felt again the surge of self-reproach and shame that he still allowed her to control him. He had backed away from the extreme demand he had thought would never come, but had not been able to make the final rejection and simply refuse to let her have Jenni Hilton's address. Everything told him he must and he persuaded himself that he could face the venom that would follow. But he was alone with no ally to support him, least of all his own wife.

"Mummy's boy been home again, has he?" Stephanie sneered as he walked into the living-room. She was curled like a cat at one end of the sofa, make-up as flawless as a girl's on a cosmetic counter; her vanity insisted that she should never look less than perfect. "No, it's not Mummy is it? It's Mum. Old Mother Kershaw, the Brentwood bitch."

He came home every night not knowing what mood she

might be in. Low-key tolerance was the most common, but she would sometimes deliberately throw him off balance with unexpected strokes of remembered warmth. This evening she was fully armed and ready for a vicious fight. A series of minor irritations had ruffled the indulgent pattern of her day; a rude shop assistant in Bond Street, her pet hairdresser unable to provide an immediate appointment, a friend who had cancelled a lunch engagement. Already frustrated by one of her lovers' increasingly suspicious excuses, a handful of little incidents had inflamed a spoiled and spiteful personality.

"Don't call her that," he replied wearily as he crossed the room to the drinks cabinet. Countless defeats had replaced anger with the sort of impotent gestures that follow retreat. "Whatever you think of her, she's still my mother. I don't ask you to get involved any more."

"No. You just let me sit at home on my own for hours," she replied petulantly. "Then expect to walk in and find a meal waiting for you."

"It's only once a week." His hand shook with tension as he held the decanter and he poured out more whisky than he had intended. He decided to drink it neat.

"Washing out the taste of her, are you? I'm not surprised. She must only have a bath once a month."

The casual, malicious barb stung him like acid hurled on an open wound. He still had his back to her, so she did not see the spasm of pain that twisted his face as he almost cried out. More clearly than the glass he was holding, he could see the glistening bathroom in Etruria Street and the image of his mother through the steam as she bent her head over the wash-basin. Her long hair had been rich chestnut then, like the princess in his best story book. Unquestioning, totally trusting love of infancy swallowed him up and only a shuddering effort stopped him turning and hurling the glass into his wife's face. Whatever else she may have been, his mother had *never* been dirty. The wracking agony began to recede, leaving an aftershock of coldness. Without another word, he walked out and Stephanie heard him cross the hall and open the door of his study. She felt no remorse at what she had said, only the sadistic satisfaction of discovering a new weapon whose torment she could use again.

As he closed the study door, Terry Kershaw gave a convulsive sob of repressed rage. For a moment, he felt dizzy, then recovered and went to the desk, taking an address book from the drawer, and looked up the home number of the owner of Insignia Motors' private inquiry agency.

"Alan? Terry Kershaw." He was surprised at how calm he sounded. "I need you to do a personal job for me—not Insignia business. I want you to find someone."

Five minutes later, after being warned that it could take time, he rang off and slumped back in his chair. It was done and now he had to rationalise it. If Jenni Hilton was found, he would tell his mother. Nothing wrong in that. If she then did something without letting him know, he could not be held responsible. And how would Stephanie cope with being the daughter-in-law of a woman who . . . No, leave that alone. Just think of it as another kind of revenge.

"Have you found anything out?" Maltravers asked as he pulled up an empty chair and sat down next to Matt Hoffman. The crime reporter turned from a story he was writing on his Atex screen and reached for a notebook.

"The fuzz admit off the record that they thought there might be something at first," he agreed. "But they couldn't make it stand up. They suspected Owen might have done it, but he was in his office doing a presentation to a client the evening his wife died. He was there with witnesses for two hours from five o'clock."

"All the time?" Maltravers interrupted. "He never left, even for a short while? It's less than five minutes' walk to Tottenham Court Road."

"If he did, then three very respectable members of one of the big five banks are telling lies. Once they started the meeting nobody left the room, not even to go for a leak. There's no way he did it."

"What about Daphne Gillie?"

"That looked more interesting for a while. She left OGM's offices at five fifteen—around her usual time—and was at the

Groucho by about six. In between she was shopping on Oxford Street."

Maltravers's interest flicked up. "Tottenham Court Road end?"

"Yep," Hoffman acknowledged. "And apparently she can't prove it. Busy shops, wandering in and out and didn't actually buy anything. All the opportunity you want—but no sign of a motive. She and Owen agreed that they plan to marry, but his wife had gotten stubborn over a divorce. On the other hand, he'd eventually be able to divorce her and she could have done nothing to stop it and they were both prepared to wait. It occurred to me she might be pregnant, but even so . . ."

"No," Maltravers interrupted. "Owen can't father children, which is why he and Caroline didn't have any. I've been told that by a friend of hers."

"It was only an idea. Anyway, when you get down to it, there's no reason on God's earth for either of them to kill Caroline Owen. She was being pig-headed over the divorce, but it wasn't a problem."

"Not pig-headed," Maltravers corrected. "Just a bad case of Roman Catholic conscience."

"Whatever." Hoffman shrugged. "The fact is that her refusal didn't matter. He's hardly tottering into his grave and she's only in her twenties. There was no panic. The police have dropped it."

Maltravers thought for a moment. The information about the police's actions was interesting but not, on the face of it, productive. "What about somebody else? Any problems with Scimitar Press?"

"Basically a one-woman business employing a couple of girls. No partners to have arguments with and the books appear to be in order."

"One of her authors?" Maltravers suggested.

Hoffman looked intrigued. "Do authors kill their publishers?"

"Not usually," Maltravers admitted. "But insanity isn't totally unknown among writers."

"Well, I didn't press on that, but as I understand it she published children's stories and books about how to grow healthy carrots." Hoffman grinned. "I like it. Dig up some organic gardener's vegetable patch and find it's being fertilised by corpses of people they fell out with. Make any front page, that would."

"OK, it was just a thought," Maltravers said. "The fact is that as far as I can make out, Caroline Owen had no enemies but now she's suddenly dead."

"From falling under a Tube train."

"But she could have been pushed."

"Yes, she could, which is exactly what the police have looked into. All they've turned up is a woman who could have done it, but she had no reason to." Hoffman closed his notebook and looked at Maltravers keenly. "Why've you got a hang-up over this?"

"She was a nice lady and it's getting to me," Maltravers answered evasively. "So are the police letting it go?"

"They've still got the inquest coming up, but that looks like being a formality. Open verdict with a few comments from the coroner about safety standards on London's Underground about which damn all will be done."

"There's still the possibility of suicide," Maltravers pointed out.

"If you can come up with a reason. The police certainly haven't found one. Anyway, you say she was a devout Catholic. Isn't suicide a mortal sin?"

"I think it is," admitted Maltravers. "She'd certainly have had to have been almost out of her mind with desperation, and from what I know she was as happy as any human being can hope to be."

"So you're left with an accident."

"Unless Daphne Gillie had a motive."

"Then you find it—and don't forget our deal. You dig up a murder out of this and I get an exclusive. See you around."

"Cheers . . . and thanks. I owe you."

Hoffman returned to his screen and Maltravers went to the coffee machine. As he waited for the plastic cup to fill, he wondered if there was anything more he could do before meeting Jack Buxton and attending the OGM party. One possibility occurred to him and he called Louella Sinclair.

"What's happening with Scimitar Press now?" he asked. "Is anyone still running it?"

"Yes. Jane Root, Caroline's pocket dynamo. Why do you want to know?"

"Perhaps she knows something without realising it. Have you met her?"

"Several times. Mention my name and tell her I say it's all right. Hang on, I'll give you the number."

Using Louella's name saved explanations, but Jane Root still sounded cautious. "You want to talk about Caroline's death? That's heavy with me at the moment."

"I appreciate that, but it could be important," Maltravers told her. "Let me buy you lunch and if it gets too painful, I'll back off."

"All right," she agreed. "You've got me interested if nothing else. The office is just round the corner from Friday's in Covent Garden. Is that all right?"

"Meet you in the foyer . . . Oh, what do you look like?"

"Small redhead. I stand out in a crowd for the wrong reasons. You'll see. About half an hour?"

Covent Garden bustled with tourists and office workers as Maltravers made his way through it. For more than three hundred years, it had been London's fruit and vegetable market, now its open-ended, glass-roofed hall contained stalls selling upmarket gifts and flower girls had been replaced by street entertainers; a music student played her flute, accompanied by amplified chamber orchestra on tape deck, a woman sang old music hall songs without any accompaniment at all, on the cobbled square outside the Palladian front of St Paul's Church two young men joked as they juggled Indian clubs deliberately badly. Maltravers walked behind them and their audience and turned down past his own publisher's offices, a tall five-storey building fitted into the terrace like one of the company's thinner volumes, and round the corner towards the Strand. Jane Root was waiting at Friday's and he recognised her immediately. She was about thirty years old and twelve years tall, lack of height compensated by crackling red hair and six foot personality. Eyes as brilliantly blue as Maltravers's own looked up at him shrewdly as they shook hands.

"I rang Louella. She says you've helped her a lot and that you'd tell me the details. Is there something wrong about Caroline's death? I mean more than the fact it happened?"

"Perhaps. I didn't think so at first, but . . . I'll tell you inside."

Friday's—properly Thank God It's Friday—is one of the places that has brought American courtesy and friendliness to London restaurants. The English, who generally don't know the difference between giving service and being servile, usually bring all the charm of a prison canteen to eating out. Being welcomed with a smile, shown to your table, offered iced water on a hot day, thoughtfully warned that some dish is unfortunately not available but something else is very good if you fancy it, having your order taken cheerfully and encouraged to enjoy your meal is not actually unknown, but is as rare for natives in London as a polite cop for New Yorkers. Within minutes, Maltravers and Jane Root had sat down, ordered, and been supplied with a bottle of decently chilled white wine.

"So what do you want to talk about?" she asked.

Maltravers glanced at her as he filled her glass. During the previous few minutes he had experienced the sense of being silently judged by a woman of sharp intelligence who would be irritated by polite prevarication.

"I think that Caroline was murdered," he told her bluntly.

"Why?" There was no emotion in the question, no horror or immediate instinct to be repulsed, just a simple demand for an explanation.

"Why do I think it or why was she?"

"Both."

"The second one I don't know." Maltravers stopped filling the glass as she indicated he had given her enough. "The first one is a long story, but I'll keep it as short as I can."

Jane Root never took her eyes off him as she listened, fingers running up and down the stem of her glass. When he finished, she pursed her mouth into a reflective *moue* for a few moments.

"First off, I can't imagine Caroline killing this character Kershaw, which is the bottom line," she said finally. "But if you and Louella think it's possible and that's why she died then I've got to look at it. She often talked about people she'd known in the Sixties, but his name never came up—which might be significant of course. If you're right, she wouldn't have wanted to talk about him. But in view of what you say he was like, I'd have remembered if she had. I'm sorry, I'd like to help you there, but I can't."

"All right, but I've also found out something else," Maltravers said. "Ted Owen's girlfriend was in the Tottenham Court Road area around the time that Caroline died . . . and I find that suspicious."

"You're not the only one."

"You mean that you do?" he asked sharply as the possibility of something showed itself. She knocked it down by confirming what Hoffman had told him.

"No, but the police do. Or did. They asked me about the affair. I told them that as far as I was aware, Caroline accepted the situation and wasn't bitter or vindictive. Really."

"But she wouldn't give him a divorce."

"Because she couldn't," Jane replied. "Don't get me wrong. Caroline wasn't a prejudiced Roman Catholic, just a very sincere one. Divorce was *wrong*. But she knew that Ted would eventually be able to divorce her and she'd have been able to cope with that. This may sound irrational, but in some ways she actually wanted the divorce herself because it would have . . . I don't know . . . closed the book. But Ted had to be the one who did it."

They were interrupted as their meal arrived and Maltravers was mixing dressing into his salad when he picked up the conversation again.

"But Louella says that Caroline told her he'd been pressing her to agree to a divorce immediately."

"That was a while back," Jane said. "Caroline never gave me any details, but I put a call from Ted through to her one afternoon and it was ages later that I went into her office and they were still talking. Well, arguing would be more like it. She was saying that she didn't care how much money was involved, there wasn't going to be a divorce. When I appeared she told him she had work to do and slammed the phone down. Then she said—"

"Money?" Maltravers interrupted. "Does he have a financial stake in Scimitar Press which would be shared out when—?"

"No," Jane cut in. "He had no connection at all. Caroline set it up and ran it on her own."

"But he mentioned money and . . . just a minute!" Maltravers's mind ran between possibilities. "What happens now she's dead? If he was her only known relative, did she . . .?"

"No." She had immediately seen how Maltravers was thinking. "The police went into that. They asked who her solicitors were so they could check her will. I told them I could save them a trip because I know what it says. Caroline told me."

"Go on."

"Caroline's only asset was Scimitar Press. She and Ted had owned their home while they were married, but when they separated, they sold it and divided the money. She used her share to launch Scimitar Press and rented somewhere to live. She kept meaning to buy a flat, but couldn't afford it. Under her will the business is to be disposed of by her lawyers and frankly won't bring in a fortune."

"But what happens to the money it does raise?" Maltravers asked.

Jane Root smiled at him curiously. "It will be split four ways. A quarter each to her local church, the Save the Children Fund, Ted . . . and me. After the legal costs, I think we'll be lucky to get about twenty thousand each top weight and that's being optimistic. A lot for the church, a welcome donation to charity and peanuts to Ted Owen. He can pull that in with his expenses."

Maltravers said nothing as he picked up the wine bottle and poured for them both again.

"You're very polite," she told him. "The police were much more inquisitive. For me twenty thousand pounds is a lot. But I'm not stupid and I'm not wicked. I wouldn't kill anyone for a bit more than a year's salary and I wouldn't have killed Caroline for all the money they've ever printed. I liked her very much and her death hurts me a lot."

"Sorry." Maltravers smiled sympathetically at the pain that crept into her eyes. "I'm detached from all this, but I've been where you are and it hurts like hell doesn't it?"

"Yes it does," she said tersely. "Any more questions?"

"None that I think you could answer, except that I interrupted you a moment ago. You were going to say that Caroline said something after putting the phone down on Ted. What was it?"

Jane Root shrugged. "It didn't make sense and I'd almost forgotten it. She was furious and . . . I can't remember the exact words, but it was something on the lines of 'Sod her bloody aunt.'"

"Aunt who?"

"I don't know. Caroline immediately asked what I wanted and obviously didn't want to talk to me about it."

Maltravers finished the last of his potato skins. "God knows what that was about. Perhaps Daphne's got some relative who wants to splash out on an expensive wedding present. Hardly enough to murder for."

"How sure are you about her being murdered? Are you sure at all?"

"No. It's just that it may tie up with this Kershaw business, but I can't see the connections."

"I can give you the names of people who'd known her longer than I had if it helps," Jane suggested.

"Louella's already on to that. Perhaps it'll turn up something."

"Where else are you looking?" she asked.

"It's all rummaging in the dark at the moment, but I'm due to meet Ted Owen and his girlfriend at an OGM party my lady's been invited to and I've fixed up a visit to someone called Jack Buxton. He's—"

"Oh, I know about Jack Buxton," she interrupted. "Caroline used to laugh herself silly remembering what a crush she had on him. He was a pop singer, wasn't he?"

"Yes . . . and tell me more. This could be important."

"Oh." She appeared surprised at the suddenly heightened interest in his voice. "I don't know much except that they had an affair twenty-odd years ago. I don't think it was a big thing, just one of those memories that Caroline treasured. What's so important about it? Caroline was quite a little raver back then. She told me about several other lovers."

"But they weren't worked over on Barry Kershaw's orders," he said grimly. "Nasty story coming up. Good job we've finished eating."

When he'd finished, Jane Root's mouth curled in disgust. "What a shit. Now I understand why you think Caroline could have been involved in killing him . . . but she just wasn't that sort of lady."

"People change," Maltravers commented. "Sometimes we look back and can hardly recognise ourselves. Anyway, Jack Buxton being beaten up and Kershaw's death were near enough to suggest one was the result of the other. If that's the case, then people who were close to Buxton become interesting. And that includes Caroline . . . and Caroline is dead."

"But there must be others," Jane argued. "Caroline told me there was a whole crowd of them in those days—and you say that plenty of them lied at Kershaw's inquest."

"True," he acknowledged. "We've only talked about Caroline because you knew her. Kershaw's death doesn't concern me. It was years ago and I accept that he deserved it. But if Caroline died because of it, I'd like to know who killed her."

"I don't like to think about that," Jane said quietly, but he heard a note of anger. "But if it's true, I hope you find them. If I come up with anything that might help, I'll let you know."

"Thank you." He gave her his phone number. "I'll keep you posted as well." He settled the bill and walked back with her to Scimitar Press.

"Has Ted Owen been in touch?" he asked. "Since Caroline died."

"No. There's no reason why he should have." They stepped round some scaffolding poles blocking half the pavement, part of London's eternal rebuilding. "He had nothing to do with the company and I can't imagine he's panting for the money he'll eventually get." They reached an anonymous door with "Scimitar Press, fifth floor" stamped on one of the plastic plates fixed to the adjacent wall. "If you'd like another coffee, you're welcome, but we're in the eyrie and and there's no lift. It's like being the doctor making house calls on Mrs Rochester."

"I'll pass at the moment, but perhaps another time."

Standing on tiptoe, she raised her face to kiss him. "I'd rather you told me it was an accident. That's bad, but not as bad as the thought of murder. She was too nice for anyone to be so cruel to her."

Chapter Eleven

Owen Graham Metcalf's launch party was infested with the humanised soap bubble, inflated by a six million pound Press and TV advertising spend designed to change the shopping and washing-up habits of Britain's housewives. Its insanely smiling face was stamped on people's lapel badges, cloths spread on buffet tables were patterned by it, swaying in the slightest draught, an immense version in clear polythene was suspended from the centre of the ceiling with matching satellite balloons in attendance. The boardroom was filled with trendily-dressed advertising people, sober-suited executives from Pearlman UK (Domestic Products Division, Accrington) plc, trying to adapt to what they regarded as an enviable metropolitan sophistication, a collection of people who could claim some tangential connection with the campaign and the inevitable boyfriends, mistresses and gatecrashers. Maltravers resisted the temptation to draw a moustache on the face of his badge's bubble logo as Tess was extravagantly embraced by the director of the television commercial and dragged off to meet Pearlman's managing director, introduced with a cry of "Mr Callaghan, this lady is the voice of Bubbles!" Maltravers hoped that Tess would behave herself and not kick him in the balls.

He made his way to a food table and helped himself to salmon roulade and fettucini with wild mushrooms and anchovies lying on a frisée of oakleaf lettuce beginning to wilt in the heat. He had just decided on Australian Chardonnay rather than Chilean Cabernet Sauvignon when somebody spoke his name. Surprised that anyone there should know him, he turned to see a man whose face he half recognised but whose name lay just beyond immediate recollection.

"Give me a clue," he said.

"*Worcester Evening Echo.*"

Maltravers paused momentarily as a series of events and journalists flashed through his mind and realisation came. "Simon . . . just a moment . . . Simon Cunliffe. What are you doing here? Don't tell me you've sold out and gone into the advertising business."

"Not quite—but I am on *Campaign* magazine which is the next worst thing. Why are you here?"

"Let's fight our way out of this lot and I'll tell you."

Holding glasses and plates at head height, they wriggled through the chattering crush and found a space by a window. Cunliffe's employers explained his presence completely. *Campaign* is the weekly Bible of British advertising. Multi-million pound accounts on the move, the rise and fall of highly paid talents, new agencies formed by people all of whom insist that their name must be included in the company's title, the creation of ingenious selling strategies provide an endless if somewhat repetitive source of news about an industry that eventually controls the lives of virtually everybody in the Western world without them realising it.

For a few minutes, the two men exchanged gossip about themselves and people they had worked with, then Maltravers glanced round the room, which appeared to be even more full than it had been when he arrived.

"Why did you bother coming tonight, though?" he asked. "Invitations to shindigs like this must be ten a penny."

"I've just done a profile on Ted Owen and his secretary called me personally," Cunliffe replied. "You know what it's like. We've reported the launch *ad nauseum*, so I didn't expect there to be any copy in it—although I've picked up a bit for the Diary page."

"What?" Maltravers was only vaguely interested until Cunliffe explained.

"Ted Owen's live-in girlfriend is wearing an engagement ring that would embarrass Liz Taylor. That's her over there near the door. Silver dress and . . ."

Maltravers looked where Cunliffe was indicating and identified Daphne Gillie, but for a few moments he did not hear anything the reporter was saying to him. Caroline Owen had been dead for only a few days and already her husband and his girlfriend had made their engagement public? It was so heartlessly repulsive that . . . He became aware that Cunliffe had started to talk about something else.

"When's the wedding?" he asked sharply.

"Whose? Oh, Ted and Daphne's. That's being kept under wraps because they don't want a fuss, but apparently it's going to be fairly soon."

"How soon is fairly soon?"

Cunliffe shrugged. "Some people think it could only be a matter of weeks. What's your interest?"

"Just that I knew Ted Owen's wife and her body's hardly bloody cold yet." Maltravers turned and looked out of the window, partly to hide his disgust, partly to prevent Cunliffe suspecting that his interest could be anything more than personal. As he did so, someone dragged Cunliffe away with standard promises of seeing him later and Maltravers was able to think by himself. Up to Caroline Owen's death, Ted and Daphne had said they were prepared to wait as long as it took before they married; now they were rushing into it as though a four-minute warning had sounded. Why? One possibility occurred to him: a wife could not give evidence against her husband and vice versa. He couldn't see that it made much sense, but Maltravers suddenly became certain that Caroline Owen's death had not been accidental and the conviction shook him. He turned back to face the room and saw Tess talking to a man with a small ponytail who must be Owen. He could leave her to deal with him while he made contact with Daphne Gillie. It took him about three quarters of an hour of meaningless conversations with other people before he managed to be alone with her by using his connection with Tess.

"She's a very good actress," Daphne Gillie said. "We had quite a job deciding which of her voices we should use."

"Did you finally choose her real one?" For a moment, he took the opportunity to elicit some information which might put Tess's mind at rest.

"No, we settled on what we called Squeaky Mark II. It was

dead right for the C1D1 target market. We'll probably want to use her again."

"She does get busy," Maltravers replied, laying the ground for what he knew would be Tess's refusal. "Have you been in the business long?"

Probing with commonplace questions gave him time to assess Daphne Gillie and he was not enchanted. Gestures and body language revealed that she used her looks as a snare; even talking to a man whom she knew was in a relationship and unlikely to be of use to her in any event, she still instinctively played the game. He carefully controlled his response—she would know if he reacted out of amusement—but still injected occasional comments that suggested he was flattered. At one point after some joke that had made her laugh, he took hold of her left hand.

"Very nice." He moved her hand and the ring sparkled. "That didn't come out of a Christmas cracker. Who's the lucky man?"

Gently but firmly, she pulled her hand away. "Ted and I have just got engaged . . . but we're not making a big thing about it. The trouble is, you can't keep anything quiet in the advertising business."

"When's the wedding?"

"Now that is a secret." She glanced over his shoulder and smiled at someone behind him. "Will you excuse me? There's somebody I must talk to. Help yourself to another drink."

It could have been a genuine ending by a polite hostess who had to spread herself among the guests, but Maltravers suspected Daphne Gillie had wanted to terminate the conversation. He spotted Tess trapped in a corner by a young man from Pearlman's, leaning with his arm against the wall to prevent her getting away; he gave the distinct impression of becoming over-excited at chatting up an attractive actress. Maltravers smoothly rescued her amid half-drunk Northern protests and steered her towards the door.

"Let's get out of here," he murmured. "I've had enough."

Outside on the pavement, they both breathed deep sighs of relief, partly at the evening coolness after the humidity of the packed room, partly at simply having escaped.

"I didn't get anything," Tess told him. "I mentioned that I

knew a friend of Caroline's to Ted Owen and sympathised over her death, but he obviously didn't want to talk about it and there was no way I could push it. How about you?"

"Oh, I picked up something, but I'm not sure what to make of it." Maltravers frowned as he glanced up and down the street. "Where did we park . . . oh yes. I'll tell you in the car because I want to go and see Louella if she's at home. Come on. Incidentally, your reputation is safe. The loathsome Bubbles will sound nothing like you."

"Oh, I know that. It was the first thing I asked Ted Owen about."

Louella Sinclair's house stood at the end of an Edwardian terrace with a view across Clapham Common; when she had bought it, such an address attracted half-amused sympathy, now it was an eminently desirable part of yuppiedom. She took Maltravers and Tess through to the front room, elegant enough for *House & Garden* (in which it had actually appeared), and heard their news with a silent dismay that bordered on revulsion.

"I knew that Ted could be a bastard," she said when they finished. "I didn't know that Daphne was such a bitch. If she dares to show her face at Caroline's funeral, I may kill."

"The question is, did they?" Maltravers observed. "I still can't see a reason, but why this rush to get married all of a sudden?"

"There's nothing to stop them now, so perhaps they just decided they may as well," Tess suggested. She did not sound convinced.

Maltravers shook his head. "If they waited a year, even six months, that would be different. But while they're keeping the actual date quiet, I have the feeling it's a damn sight sooner than that. And they must know that anyone who was a friend of Caroline's would be offended. So what's so important that they're prepared to live with what people are going to think?"

"They probably don't give a damn," Louella said. "But it's as though they're deliberately going out of their way to upset people. What for?"

"There has to be something and giving offence is hardly enough." Maltravers looked at Louella. "I've been thinking it over as we drove here and keep stumbling because the starting point could somehow be that party when Kershaw died. Jenni and Caroline were both there and could have been mixed up in his death. You say Ted wasn't among the guests, that he didn't know him, but he could have met Kershaw sometime and you know nothing about it. That at least brings everyone together."

"All right, but where does it get us?" she demanded in exasperation. "That was 1968 for God's sake. Caroline and I stopped talking about Barry Kershaw a long time ago and Ted certainly never mentioned him. The only thing you've told me that's happening now is that Jenni asked you to take his name out of your profile of her . . . When's that appearing?"

"Tomorrow—and Kershaw's been deleted. The trouble is that he's dead but he won't lie down. The evil that men do may surely live after them."

"Well, there was no bloody good interred with his bones," Louella remarked caustically. "I've managed to contact a couple of people from the old days, but they're scattered all over the place now. They were intrigued, but had no suggestions. I didn't bother with Jack Buxton because you're seeing him."

"That's tomorrow as well," Maltravers confirmed. "I shall be a person in, rather than from, Porlock. Bad day for Coleridge that. Perhaps I'll have more luck."

The winding-up of OGM's party had been carefully arranged in advance. Male Pearlman employees determined to sample Soho's salacious delights—which they were erroneously convinced would offer more blatant bawdiness than similar clubs back home—had been taken to an establishment which would sell them cheap champagne at two hundred pounds a bottle in return for ultimate disappointment, and the chairman and his wife had been escorted to the Talk of the Town for less expensive drinks and better entertainment. Ted Owen told one of his executives to make sure the last drunken hangers-on were flushed out of the building as he and Daphne Gillie were leaving. She sank back in the front seat of the Mercedes with relief and spoke with her eyes closed.

"Cynthia disappeared with Dudley, Linda and Mick vanished after half an hour, Sophie was almost undressing Alan as they went to the lift and Dennis couldn't keep his eyes off young Paul all evening. Everybody appears to be changing beds."

Owen turned up towards Euston Road and the longer but quieter route from the West End to Richmond, accelerating to beat an amber light. "Did Tess Davy talk to you?"

Daphne turned her head against the padded support behind her seat and looked at him. "No. Why do you ask?"

"She was asking me about Caroline."

"What about her?" She sat up, abruptly reanimated out of post-party exhaustion.

"Nothing in particular. Just that she knows Louella Sinclair, an old friend of Caroline's, and that Caroline used to be a publisher's editor for her boyfriend. What's his name? Guy?"

"Gus. Gus Maltravers. He was talking to me at one point."

"Did he mention Caroline?"

"No, but he made some comment about my engagement ring. Asked when the wedding was going to be. What did you say to Tess Davy?"

"Stupid bastard!" They lurched against their seat belts as Owen braked to avoid hitting a delivery van cutting him up. He flashed his headlights angrily as he swerved past. "I didn't say anything. Gave her a touch of the grieving husband bit and changed the subject. It just seemed strange she should bring it up. Not the sort of thing I'd have expected her to mention in the circumstances."

Daphne relaxed again. "Sympathetic small talk. Nothing to worry about."

"What about Maltravers asking about the wedding?"

"Same thing," she said dismissively. "He wasn't the only one." She held out her hand, fingers spread wide, and street-lamps fired the diamond with orange shafts of passing light. "Perhaps we should have chosen something less outrageous. But when you've got it, flaunt it."

Terry Kershaw took the call from the detective agency in his study again.

"Drawn a blank so far. Tried the *Daily Express*, but they say they don't know where she lives and there's nothing else to go on. I've got someone making inquiries at the theatre and we're asking taxi drivers in the area. One of them may have taken her home. Apart from that, it's needle in a haystack country. When do you want this by?"

"Soon as you can," Kershaw replied. "If I come up with anything else that could help, I'll pass it on. Keep me posted. Cheers."

After starting the process of tracing Jenni Hilton, Kershaw had at first started moving back towards the idea that telling his mother would be to collude with her obsession. Self-determination fatally undermined by two possessive women, he had swayed between what his conscience said he should do, what confused loyalties urged him to do, and what a desire to hit back at his wife tempted him to do. Finally he had decided to try and find the information and then think again. The eventual decision would be a matter of chance, depending on who manipulated him and in which direction. Successful in business, popular with friends, Terry Kershaw was privately tormented by the acceptance of his own weakness and a recognition that he was unable to do anything about it. He could not even draw strength from the fear that a woman's life could depend on which way he allowed himself to be pushed.

Chapter Twelve

Pictured half in shadow against the curtains of her front room, Jenni Hilton's four-column image on the front page of *The Chronicle*'s Weekend section encapsulated distance and mystery. A less skilled photographer would have captured preserved beauty; a vainer and less intelligent woman would have insisted that he did so. Instead, the loveliness was there only to be seen by those who looked carefully. Maltravers gave the illustration a nod of silent admiration, then grimaced slightly at the headline drawn from a Beatles classic: WHY SHE HAD TO GO, I DON'T KNOW, SHE WOULDN'T SAY. It highlighted an aspect of his piece he would rather they had played down. Non-journalists often imagine that writers produce their own headlines, unaware that sub-editors jealously guard that privilege, now enhancing with brilliance, now damaging with awfulness. Taking as detached a view as he could, Maltravers had to admit the head cleverly caught a central point about Jenni Hilton, complete with an appropriate Sixties' flavour, but wished they had come up with something else. He automatically checked that any reference to Barry Kershaw had been deleted, which it had.

"You shouldn't look so smug about your own work," Tess told him as he read a passage again. "It's conceited."

"I'm allowed a little satisfaction over doing my job well, and I know better than anyone else where it could have been improved. That bit's sloppy." He folded the paper and dropped it on the floor by the kitchen table. "Anyway, there's nothing that Jenni Hilton can complain about. No mention of Kershaw."

"She might worry if she knew what we were up to," Tess remarked.

"All we're trying to discover is why Caroline Owen died with nothing more to go on than a gut feeling she was murdered. It's nothing to do with Jenni . . ." He paused as a new thought occurred to him, "Unless, of course, she has or had some connection with Ted Owen. Did you raise that when you spoke to him?"

"No," Tess sighed. "That's the problem isn't it? I woke up during the night and lay awake for ages trying to make connections."

"Well, I'm not about to make some runic Poirot-style comment revealing that I've worked out something everyone else has missed. Irritating habit." He stood up. "All I have is the possibility that Porlock might produce something more than another piece *The Chronicle* will pay me for."

Tess pouted mischievously. "I was rather hoping for a dirty weekend as well."

"Dirty weekends are illicit. We shall have a clean weekend. Same basic principle, considerably less screwing."

She wrinkled her nose at him. "I'll settle for that."

"Sensualist. But don't forget we're after information. You grill Kate Buxton to see if she knows anything while I work on her husband."

Maltravers and Tess left London so early that they were speeding past Bristol when Kershaw called the detective agency again.

"Have you seen this morning's *Chronicle*? There's a feature about Jenni Hilton."

"We'll get hold of a copy. I take it there's no address."

"Not even a district. Call them and see if they'll tell you."

"There'll be nobody in on a Saturday. Who wrote it?"

"Someone called . . . Augustus Maltravers. Doesn't say anything about him though."

"Spell it . . . hang on." Kershaw heard the phone being laid down and there were a few moments of silence before it was picked up again. "This could be handy. There's only one Maltravers in the London phone book. Initial A. Lives in Coppersmith Street. It's certainly worth a try. I'll call you back."

Kershaw replaced the receiver and almost instantly it rang. It was his mother. Yes, he had seen *The Chronicle.* Yes, he was on to it. Yes, the agency was trying to . . . Yes, Mum. Yes, Mum . . . All right, Mum. Yes, Mum. "No" had always been a difficult word.

Stephanie walked in just as he managed to end the conversation. She was pulling on a pair of string-backed driving gloves and he could smell the Giorgio Beverly Hills perfume he had bought for her birthday.

"I'm going shopping." Shopping in a Chanel suit, perfume worth a hundred and fifty pounds and Gucci shoes. "I'll probably be late back. The girls are spending the day with the Weinrebs. You can find something for lunch in the fridge."

"What time will you be back?"

She smoothed the gloves against her hands and examined the results critically. "Expect me when you see me. I may pop in to Mummy and Daddy's . . . or go to someone who's invited me round for a drink."

She was gone. No goodbye, no kiss, not even the gesture of a casual wave. Terry Kershaw heard the front door slam and gravel scatter as the Mercedes skidded away from the house. The phone rang again and he picked it up like an automaton.

"It's Alan Bedford again. Maltravers is out. I've left a message on the ansaphone. There's no guarantee he's the right one, but it's a reasonable chance. When we get the paper, we'll see if he's dropped any clues."

"I couldn't see anything," Kershaw said. "I think she's being secretive."

"We'll find her. Nobody can hide in London for ever. Just be patient. Cheers, Terry . . ."

"No, hang on! There's something else." Kershaw realised he was gripping the receiver tighter as months of vague suspicions came into focus. "This is right off the record, Alan. Just between you and me. Nothing at all to do with Insignia. No talking to the old man."

"You know my company well enough, Terry. All confidentialities are respected. As long as everything's above board. What is it?"

"I want you to follow my wife."

There was a pause. "I see. How long for?"

"As long as it takes to find out where she spends her time when I'm at work."

"I'm . . . sorry you're asking me to do that. It wasn't the sort of thing I thought would happen in your case. Anyway, when would you like us to begin?"

"Today. She says she's gone shopping for the day. She doesn't think anywhere but Harrods exists. If she goes there, you should pick her up."

"There'll be a young lady at your house in about twenty minutes," Bedford told him. "Let her have a recent photograph and she'll take it from there. As soon as we have anything, I'll let you know."

Jack and Kate Buxton's guesthouse stood near the bottom of the nerve-wrackingly steep Porlock Hill and the air outside carried the smell of burning brake pads as unprepared tourists descended it for the first—and what they probably swore would be the last—time. Shining white pebble-dash walls with flowered curtains glimpsed through diamond leaded windows and thick overhanging thatch provided the ideal vision for holidaymakers, particularly Americans, seeking a romanticised version of England. Inside were pieces of genuine Georgian furniture, embroidered cloths on occasional tables in the lounge, crocheted linen antimacassars on plump easy chairs and sepia hunting prints which filled the walls. The overall combination was historically ridiculous, but offered a restful idiosyncratic style with the added comforts of contemporary plumbing and colour television.

Jack Buxton's face was still recognisable from the photographs that Maltravers had seen while doing his research, but swollen with years and what had been obligatory, rebellious long hair replaced by a diminishing cap of ash grey, brushed forward like a worn mop. As they shook hands, Maltravers felt as though he had taken hold of a large knuckle end of pork, dead flesh distorted by a jumble of bone. He could not help looking down at reddened fingers twisted with chronic arthritis, erupting out of palms like mangled giant prawns.

"If you know about me, you know about them," Buxton said.

"I know," Maltravers acknowledged sympathetically. "Will you mind talking about that?"

"No. I've learned to live with it. Anyway, you'll want to freshen up first. I'll show you your room—sorry, I can't carry cases."

They followed him up narrow stairs to the first floor. Whatever Jasmine Cottage had originally been built as, it had been large and the upper floor was divided into six double bedrooms. Buxton let them into one at the back.

"There's less noise from the traffic here," he said, glancing round proprietorially to make sure some chambermaid had done her job properly. "Sorry, that soap should have been replaced. I'll deal with it. If there's anything else you want, call me or Kate. When you're ready you'll find me downstairs."

There was no bathroom en suite, so Tess went to find one while Maltravers unpacked what few clothes they had brought and he was reading a tourists' guide to Exmoor when she returned twenty minutes later.

"Other end of the corridor." she told him. "Very swish. I'll go down and introduce myself to Kate Buxton while you shower. If she was a dancer, there's a chance she may have known some people I've met who are still in the business. That should get us going."

"Good luck."

Maltravers checked his tape recorder before going downstairs; it was an invaluable invention for his profession, but he constantly feared it would go wrong in mid-interview and he would not have the remotest idea how to fix it. A couple of tests persuaded him that its inner mysteries were still functioning and he went to find Buxton, who was leaning against the reception desk reading *The Chronicle*.

"Is this how you got on to me?" he asked. "Through Jenni."

"Indirectly," Maltravers said. "Because of that, I met Louella Sinclair and she told me about you."

"Louella? God, you're going back." Recollection half rueful, half painful crossed Buxton's face. "I had it all going for me in those days. This interview could rake up an awful lot."

"I hope it does . . . Where's the best place to talk?"

"We'll use the lounge." Buxton stepped round from behind the desk. "It's only available to guests in the evening."

"Where's Tess?" Maltravers asked as he followed him.

"In the kitchen talking to Kate. It's like old home week in there. Swapping gossip as though Kate had never left the business."

Satisfied that Tess had made a start, Maltravers began his interview with a handful of open-ended questions which allowed Buxton to relax while he recounted the story of his career and subsequent success. He began to chainsmoke, cigarettes held with clumsy skill. Little came out that Maltravers did not already know, and it flowed smoothly until Buxton held up his hands.

"Then I had to quit." He stopped abruptly, eyes stained with what must have been constant physical pain. "Do you want to know how it happened?"

"I already know most of it. Barry Kershaw."

"You've got it." Buxton stubbed out a cigarette and immediately lit another. "Nobody could prove anything though. He covered all his tracks. How much of the story have you dug up?"

"Check this out," Maltravers replied and ran through what Louella Sinclair had told him.

"Then you know," Buxton acknowledged. "The bastard left me with no way back. So I end up here. Some of the older guests recognise me from time to time, but apart from that it's as though none of it ever happened."

"How bitter are you?"

Buxton shrugged. "Not as much as I was. Bitterness burns you up. Two things helped. Kate marrying me despite my being semi-crippled—and Kershaw buying it."

Maltravers reached across the low table between them and stopped the tape. "Let's go off the record for a minute. Louella is convinced Kershaw was murdered."

"Of course he was."

"Who by? This is just you and me now."

"I tried to find out, but either nobody knew or they weren't saying." Buxton smiled sourly. "Pity. I wanted to thank them."

"Educated guess?"

"I wouldn't know where to start." Buxton glanced at him suspiciously. "If you can't use any of this, why are you interested?"

"Curiosity. Professional habit."

"Balls."

Maltravers grinned. He remembered Louella telling him about Buxton's intelligence and decided it would be better to own up.

"OK, I'll come clean. The interview's genuine—you can ring *The Chronicle* and check that if you want—but there is more to it. Answer one more question, then I'll tell you. When were you last in London?"

"Sometime in March, certainly before Easter. Once the season starts we never get away from here." Buxton's eyes hardened. "There's your answer. You're on next."

"If you've been here all that time, you can't have had anything to do with Caroline Owen's death. That's when all this sprang up again."

"Caroline? I didn't know she was dead." Buxton leant forward, closing the already narrow space that separated them. "Explanations, friend."

For a quarter of an hour, he remained silent as Maltravers explained everything that had happened and what he suspected but could make no sense of.

"I can understand why you wanted to see me," Buxton acknowledged at the end. "But you could have been upfront from the start. The interview excuse wasn't necessary."

"I wasn't to know that," Maltravers pointed out. "The only way of finding out what you were like was to meet you personally. Now I know, I can be . . . less devious. Got any thoughts?"

"I remember Caroline very well," Buxton said. "We had a thing going for a while, but it fizzled out like a lot of others. If this Owen guy was anything to do with Kershaw, it's news to me. Someone told me Caroline was married, but I never met him. As for Jenni . . ." Maltravers waited while he lit another cigarette. He had left an interval of almost five minutes since the last one. "She was the one I nearly married."

"What happened?" This was new information. Buxton's

name had come up among others when Maltravers and Jenni Hilton had talked over lunch after the interview, but she had not indicated there had been anything special about the relationship. As far as he could remember, she had almost been dismissive.

"The easy answer is that Kate happened. But it was more complicated than that. For Jenni we were Romeo and Juliet at maximum volume, but . . . I don't know. Either her fire was too hot or mine started to go out. We'd kept it quiet for some reason—can't remember why now, perhaps it just added to the excitement—but I wanted out. I'd met Kate and she was my big thing—she still is. But I never cheated on Jenni. When I knew I had to end it, I was straight up." He gave a small laugh with little humour in it. "Asked her to meet me for a drink, thanked her, told her how sorry I was. I really tried to do it right."

Maltravers frowned. "When was this?"

"Eighteenth of June, 1968. In a pub at Kew. Can see it now."

"Less than two weeks after Kershaw died and the day before she walked off that film set . . ." The answer to a critical question suddenly appeared. "So were *you* the reason she wouldn't tell me about?"

"Come on," Buxton protested. "Jenni was too level-headed to chuck in a career like she had because of a broken heart. Obviously I thought there was a connection at first, but I expected her to turn up after a couple of weeks with some cover story about a breakdown. When she never came back, it had to be something more than carrying a torch for me. You can't pin that disappearance on Jack Buxton."

"But if not that, then what?" Maltravers demanded. "Whatever the ultimate reason may have been, when she did a runner she was crying over you in the wee, small hours."

"So she got the blue meanies playing Sinatra. We've all had them and they make us do funny things. But you get over them." Buxton shook his head. "No way. There had to be something else."

There was a long silence before Maltravers reached an answer that shook him with its plausibility.

"How about this? Jenni Hilton killed Kershaw—and she did it for you. Then you finished with her. The man she loved enough to murder for. That was something she'd have wanted to run a long way away from." He gave a long, heavy sigh out of years of private adoration. Uttering something unthinkable gave it substance. "Jesus H. Christ."

"Come on." There was instant rejection and disbelief in Buxton's voice. "What are you trying to lay on me here?"

"You knew nothing about it," Maltravers told him. "But try and knock it down. I can't."

"Jenni wasn't . . . She wouldn't have hurt a fly."

"She didn't hurt a fly. She killed a . . . I don't know . . . a five-star bastard from everything I've been told. And she did it out of love. Jack, for reasons I won't bore you with, I like the idea of Jenni Hilton murdering someone as little as you do. But after what you've told me, I can't make it go away."

"All right so I'll admit it's possible," Buxton agreed reluctantly. "Sick, but possible. What do we do about it?"

"Regarding Kershaw, damn all. Suddenly we have a theory, but there's no proof—and let's face it, we could both persuade ourselves that it was justifiable. You more than anyone. The only thing that interests me about Kershaw is how he ties in with Caroline's death."

"You're not suggesting Jenni did that as well, are you?"

Maltravers hesitated before replying. "That was just a pause for thought. No, because it doesn't make sense. The only explanation would be that Caroline knew Jenni was the murderer and had been blackmailing her and that's crap. Caroline wasn't like that and why should Jenni kill her after years of paying her off? The link's got to be somewhere else."

"So are you back with Ted Owen?" Buxton asked. "You say that nobody knows of any connection between him and Kershaw . . . unless Jenni does."

"And she certainly won't tell me . . . Would she tell you?"

"Don't count on it. If she murdered Barry—I'm not sure how far I go along with that, but still—if she did, she never told me. And that could have been a way of holding on to me."

"I can't imagine Jenni would have wanted you on terms like that," Maltravers replied. "Not after you'd told her it was over . . . Look we can finish the interview later. You must have worked out that Tess is more than just casually chatting to

Kate. Sorry about the deceit, but now you know the reason. Let's go and explain and we can all talk together."

Buxton checked his watch. "After dinner? We don't serve it, but there are a couple of restaurants in the village that we recommend. In the meantime, I've got a business to run and I left the Sixties a long time back—until you arrived."

Chapter Thirteen

Before she left for Exeter on Saturday morning to see Russell, Jenni Hilton received several calls congratulating her on Maltravers's feature. People she had maintained contact with from her professional days envied her the free publicity, those who led unpublic lives were impressed and vaguely surprised that someone they knew as a friend should be able to attract such extensive coverage in a newspaper. One call was from a film producer. He was trying to raise the finance to make *Love in the Time of Cholera* and the role of Fermina Daza still hadn't been cast . . . She was startled that her reputation had survived a twenty-year hiatus at such a level. She adored the book and the role offered the opportunity for a stupendous comeback. She promised to think about it and realised when the call was finished how much she wanted to do it. But it was too high profile, a major production that would include a massive publicity drive, appearances on television chat shows, endless interviews. Her contract would mean she would have to become public property again, every shred of her privacy lost until there were no hiding places. Was playing Márquez's eternally pursued heroine worth it? Who would play Florentino Ariza? Both parts aged over sixty years or so, they would have to split them between actors. Say Harry Connick Jnr—or perhaps Emilio Estevez—for the young version and . . . Jack Nicholson for the old man? No; Raul Julia would be perfect. She'd have no problem with the middle-aged woman and could tackle the old one, but what about the young girl? Sandrine Bonnaire? Julia Roberts? Or would Meryl Streep want to go from teenage to the end of life in a South American accent from her collection? Perhaps . . .

"Stop it!" she shouted at herself. "It's out of the question!"

But was it? Agreeing to an interview in a national newspaper was the same as admitting you had deliberately made yourself pregnant, but only a little bit. It was the start of a process that was difficult to control unless you stopped it completely. And Fermina Daza . . . she went to the bookcase and found the book, flicking through its pages. Who would be doing the screen adaptation? As she read, she could feel lines on her lips. Where would they shoot? Mexico? Brazil? A long end shot of the riverboat endlessly sailing to an Amazonian Avalon? Plaintive notes of a violin—perhaps mixed with a nose flute—and . . .

No. She replaced the book abruptly. She would be prepared to take on the occasional supporting role on television if it was offered, some radio work, provincial theatre, sufficient to feed a renewed desire, anonymous enough to be safe. But she could never go back to being the star she had been. Fame at that level held too many dangers of discovery.

Just an address, Terry. You can't refuse me that. Not after all this time, not after all I've done for you. Then you can forget about it, just leave it with me. You'll never know anything, unless . . . No, don't think about unless. All it needs is a plan. Barry was good at plans. He was always telling me about his plans. What would Barry have done? Not that he'd ever do anything like this because he was a good boy and never had to. But if he had . . . Find if she lives on her own or with one of her fancy men. Ask a neighbour. Probably lives in a snooty area where they don't chat to you like some of them round here. So pretend you're looking for somebody. Think of some story. Perhaps the daily will answer the door and she'll talk. Then get into the house. How? Too old to break in, use your common, Maureen. Think. Where's that paper got to? There was something about . . . Where's my glasses? Let's see . . . here it is. Belongs to the World Wide Fund for Nature and Save the Whales. Typical. So, just knock on the door and ask . . . need to be careful. Must look right, make her think I'm genuine. It'll only need a moment to get in, then . . .

How? Weapon? Maggie Crisp's eldest has guns. Been in

trouble for them. But he'd ask questions and remember afterwards. Couldn't shoot the thing anyway. She's young as well, her picture shows that. Have to surprise her . . . something quick. Want to get away with it as well. No point in going to Holloway if you can avoid it. Doreen Smith went in there after that fight down the Dockers Arms in 1947 when she slashed that slag's face with a broken stout bottle. Said it smelt. Wouldn't like that. Worry about that later. Weapon . . . weapon. That carving knife wouldn't cut butter. Buy a new one from that ironmongers on the High Street. Saw some in the window the other week. Cheap rubbish though, not like they used to make . . . Just a minute. Where did that bayonet get to? The one that Barry came home with one day when he was a nipper. Said he found it down the corporation tip and cleaned it up. He loved that. Hung on the wall of his room for years. He sharpened it as well, didn't he? Did Terry ever have it? No, it got put in one of those boxes with Barry's other things when we left Etruria Street. Must be in the back bedroom with the other stuff that never got thrown out. That's it. Barry's bayonet. Couldn't be better. It would be like having him there, like him killing her somehow. Just the address, Terry. Just the address.

Maltravers and Tess left Porlock after breakfast on Sunday morning and decided to drive up to Dunkery Beacon before returning. It was obviously going to be as hot in Somerset as it had been in London, but high on hills blotched with claret-coloured heather it was a promise, not a threat. They left the car and walked across the moorland to look across Exton Vale.

"Hardy found this brooding." Maltravers commented as they gazed across bright, morning-fresh landscape. "But he always had that streak of misery in him. After all, he was an architect."

Tess gave a sympathetic smile. "Joking to cover your feelings? The idea that Jenni Hilton could be a murderer got to you, didn't it?"

"More than it should have done," he admitted. "Stupid, isn't it? Teenage emotions tormenting me when I'm turned forty."

"You'll still be a romantic when you're ninety." Tess hesitated. "Can you hack it?"

"Of course I can. I'll just go into detached, journalistic mode.

That doesn't allow you to be emotional . . . but it makes you critical." He shaded his eyes as he looked towards where the sun was still yellowing lapis lazuli sky. "It adds up. She loved Jack Buxton, Kershaw had him savagely attacked, she killed in revenge. Then Jack finished with her. She ran away. No holes in that reasoning and if that was all there was to it, there'd be no problem. From what I've been told, I don't give a damn about Kershaw. He was a bastard and there's an end on't . . . but Caroline Owen wasn't like that."

"And neither Jack nor Kate could come up with anything special between her and Kershaw, and they'd never even heard of Ted Owen until we mentioned him." Tess kicked a tuft of gorse. "Not the most satisfactory weekend."

"Oh, I don't know." Maltravers squeezed her hand. "Last night had its moments. Let's see if the comatose state induced by the M4 bubbles anything out of the subconscious."

Aggravated by roadworks and a dead car transporter, the motorway was more likely to induce a nervous breakdown than inspiration. Having gone through imaginative variations on a wide vocabulary of obscenities, Maltravers abandoned it at Reading, recovered his temper over beer and a good ploughman's lunch (the only immortal sales gimmick to come out of the transitory world of advertising) at Thame and was restored to the state of human being rather than homicidal maniac trapped in a steel box on wheels by the time they reached Coppersmith Street. As Tess opened post that had arrived after their departure on Saturday, he turned on the ansaphone for the one message it contained.

"My name's Alan Bedford. I'm not sure if I've got the right number, but if you're the Augustus Maltravers who wrote the article about Jenni Hilton in today's *Chronicle*, could you call me on 071 956 1485? Sorry to have troubled you if I've got it wrong. Goodbye."

"Who's Alan Bedford?" Tess asked as she threw away another offer of a personal pensions plan.

Maltravers picked up the phone. "Never heard of him. Wonder how he got my number? *The Chronicle* certainly wouldn't have given it out. There are standard rules about that. They'd have just taken his number and offered to pass it on to

. . . Hello, Mr Bedford? Augustus Maltravers. You left a message."

"Oh, yes. Thank you for calling. First of all, have I got the right person?"

"Yes, but I'm intrigued as to how you found me."

"Telephone directory. There's no one else in it with your name, so it was worth a try. Anyway, now that I've found you, I want to ask something about your feature on Jenni Hilton. Is it possible to let me have her address?"

"Why do you want it?" Maltravers silently beckoned Tess to stand close to him so that she could hear Bedford's end of the conversation.

"Somebody's asked me to try and find it."

"That's only half an answer, Mr Bedford. Who?"

"I'm not at liberty to say that."

"And I'm not at liberty to tell you anything," Maltravers told him tersely. "Miss Hilton has strictly requested that her address be kept secret—and even if she hadn't, I certainly wouldn't give it to some stranger who rings up out of the blue talking in riddles."

"If I've offended you, Mr Maltravers, I apologise," Bedford said. "I should have explained at the beginning. I run a private inquiry agency. Perfectly legitimate, we advertise our services in the Law Society's *Gazette*. Much of our work is for the courts and I could refer you to very senior Scotland Yard officers who will vouch for me. I have been asked to obtain this information for a client and you'll appreciate that confidentiality is essential in my business. I cannot tell you who it is."

Maltravers's mind raced with new and disturbing questions. "Is it a man or a woman?"

"I can't even tell you that. It's a client. One who uses our services regularly."

"Do you have any idea what you may be messing about with, Mr Bedford?"

"I'm not aware that I'm messing about with anything. I have simply been asked to try and find where someone lives. For all I know, she may be a bad debtor. If you're unable to tell me, I'll have to continue inquiries elsewhere. Sorry to have troubled you."

"Can I come and see you?"

"If you wish. Our offices are just off the City Road. The phone's switched through to my home when we're closed. But I'm not going to tell you who I'm working for."

"I realise that. But I may be able to tell you something. I'll be in touch."

"Goodbye, Mr Maltravers."

Tess stared at him as he rang off. "What the hell was that about?"

"Christ knows. He's an inquiry agent who's been asked to find where Jenni Hilton lives. He sounds straight enough. Gives his phone number, offers references. But who's he working for? And why do they want to know her address? If it was a fan or a friend from way back, they could write to her care of *The Chronicle* and they'd send the letter on. They wouldn't use a private detective. That's . . . sly."

"Are you going to let her know? He said he'd make other inquiries. Could it be dangerous if he finds her and passes it on?"

"I can't at the moment, she's in Exeter until Wednesday. I'll go and see this Bedford character tomorrow and spell out a few facts. That might make him think twice." Maltravers shook himself in irritation. "What the fuck is going on here?"

"Ted Owen's the type who could hire a private detective." Tess glanced at him questioningly. "Don't you think?"

"Yes, he is," he agreed. "But that's just shooting in the dark. It could equally well be someone we've never heard about. Louella said there were—how many was it?—certainly a fair number of people at Kershaw's last party. It could be any one of them. God alone knows what this feature's stirred up. Jesus, the power of the Press."

The photographic power of the Press, coupled with a passenger casually leaving his newspaper in a taxi, actually betrayed where Jenni Hilton lived. Bedford's contacts among London's cabbies were considerable and had frequently repaid the monies he had distributed among them. Waiting for a fare late on Sunday evening, one driver started to read *The Chronicle* he had found on the back seat; it was not his usual sort of paper, but it had racing in it. Separating out the Weekend section, he first saw the picture and then his eyes caught the name. One of Bedford's legmen had been asking about her, but had not been able to provide a picture; now it all clicked into place. He'd picked her up in . . . St Martin's Lane it had been . . . a week or so back and half recognised her face. There was nothing special about driving the most famous of fares—it happened all the time—but she'd stuck in his mind because he'd not quite been able to place her. She'd been alone, so there had been no conversation he could listen to for a clue. But he remembered where he'd dropped her, watching her open the front door as he turned round, still trying to identify her. Could be worth a few bob from Alan Bedford—and there was a phone box just across the road. His fare had asked him to hang on, even with the meter running, and there was no sign he was coming yet. Earn a bit more while I'm waiting.

Daphne Gillie was in a teasing mood, wriggling away coquettishly as Ted Owen laughingly tried to grab hold of her. She would have been unrecognisable to OGM employees who referred to her as Madame Ceausescu.

"Get *off*!" She squirmed as he squeezed her breasts. "You can't have it. It's too hot."

"No it isn't," he contradicted as she struggled free. "Come here . . . mind that chair!"

Half deceived, she glanced round and he pounced on her, both of them rolling across the carpet like children until he pinned her wrists on the white bearskin rug in front of the fireplace. She kept resisting for a few seconds, then willing surrender and desire burned in her eyes and she licked her lips provocatively. He relaxed his grip.

"Bully." She wrapped her arms around his neck. "Big bully . . . rich bully . . . gorgeous bully. Here. Now."

She pulled his head down, fiercely pressing hungry mouths together, coquette become whore. As they writhed on the soft white pile, each freeing eager flesh from the other's clothing, a draught from an open window blew a sheet of Saturday's *Chronicle* off the sofa on to the floor. Both of them had commented on the appearance of Jenni Hilton so soon after Caroline had died.

It was very sharp. Barry had done that. She remembered him borrowing his dad's Carborundum stone and sitting for hours on the kitchen step into the back yard at Etruria Street, endlessly running it along the bayonet's edge, scraping the blade gently with his thumb to test its sharpness. Discovering it at the bottom of the box had been like a sign from Barry. Go for it, Mum. You're right, Mum, you always were right. Find her and do it. Just tell me the address, Terry. Your brother wants you to do that as well. After that, your Mum'll take care of it. You and Stephanie can just get on with your lives.

Chapter Fourteen

"We've found where Jenni Hilton lives, Terry. Twelve Cheyne Street, Chelsea." Bedford had decided it was too late to pass on the taxi driver's information when he received it on Sunday evening and called first thing on Monday.

Terry Kershaw experienced a faint feeling of numbness. He was finding it difficult to think straight in an emotional confusion of suspicion about his wife and terrifying demands from his mother.

"Thanks, Alan." He wrote the address down and stared at it for a moment. "What about the other business? About Stephanie."

"Nothing to report on Saturday. If she was at Harrods or in the Knightsbridge area, our girl certainly didn't see her. There are two of them on it now and I'll let you know as soon as we have anything. All right?"

"Yes fine . . . Oh, and send your bill for Jenni Hilton made out to me at my home. Mark it private and personal. I'll expect to hear from you."

Bedford rang off and looked at the file for Terry Kershaw's newly opened private account on his desk. Although he had made sympathetic noises when Kershaw had asked him to follow his wife, frankly he had not been surprised. The first time he had met Stephanie Kershaw—only for a few minutes at the office—he had known instantly she was spoiled, callous and self-centred. It was usually wives wanting husbands watched, but the reason was always the same. The Jenni Hilton business appeared to be something different, and Bedford made a note that the invoice was to be a personal one, which meant it was not an Insignia Motors matter. That was unexpected, but if Terry Kershaw wanted to trace her and couldn't be bothered or didn't have the time to do it himself, there was nothing to be concerned about on the face of it, although . . . Bedford read the notes he had made when he spoke to Maltravers, remembering how serious he had sounded when he suggested there was something unspecified the agency could be becoming mixed up in. If Maltravers came to see him, he would presumably say more; in the meantime, it was a pencilled-in question mark, a reminder to be cautious. Bedford's Inquiry Agency did not put its reputation at risk by undertaking work about which there were any doubts, however well-established and apparently honest the client happened to be.

In his office at Insignia Motors, Terry Kershaw repeatedly drew a frame round the address as he tried to decide what he should do. Simply lying to his mother that Jenni Hilton remained untraceable would be bottling out, a means of avoiding the fury that blank refusal would bring. But she would not let it go—she had never let it go—and eventually there would be no excuses left. Suspicion that he was deceiving her would harden into conviction until she challenged him, twisting his feelings, relentlessly torturing him with bitter accusations of disbelief at his betrayal. Could he resist that?

Caroline Owen's funeral took place on Monday morning. Louella Sinclair spotted Ted the moment she entered the church and flinched with rage when she saw that a woman was sitting next to him in the front pew. Had Daphne Gillie really dared to show her face at . . . but then the woman turned to speak to him and Louella recognised Jane Root. Having sat down and bowed her head in private prayers containing no conviction of the company of countless saints or Resurrection by the Son—wearing a hat had been her only concession to a religious faith which she and Caroline had stopped arguing over years ago—she looked round. The service was due to start in a few minutes and it seemed that Caroline had attracted about fifty people to make their farewells; not a bad average for a woman with a small family. Apart from Ted and Jane, there was nobody Louella recognised, nobody who looked as though they were the middle-aged version of some half-forgotten youthful face from the Sixties. Pity. That could have offered the opportunity to probe other memories; she had only been able to trace two people from the old days.

As soft organ music played and latecomers discreetly made their way in, Louella thought over what Maltravers had told her when he phoned after the visit to Porlock. His suggestion that Jenni Hilton could have killed Barry had not shocked her; she had always been convinced that somebody had done it, why not Jenni? She may have been one of those people cloaked in the public's belief that the famous are different, somehow protected from everyday reality, but behind the glitter of their lifestyle, they were like everybody else. Fame offered no magic shield against life's pressures and insistences.

There was a movement to her right and she looked round to see that Maltravers and Tess had joined her.

"Hello," he whispered. "All right?"

"Just about. I'm glad there's somebody here I know."

"We'll get through it." He squeezed her hand and smiled and Tess reached across him to do the same.

"Have you done anything about that detective who is trying to find Jenni?" Louella asked softly.

"I'm going to see him after this and try to find out what's going on. I don't like . . ."

Maltravers stopped as the voice of the priest began to speak from behind them and the coffin was carried down the aisle and laid on trestles in front of the altar. The six bearers—employees of the funeral director who had never met Caroline—stood with solemnly bowed heads and clasped hands for a moment of meaningless salutation to another anonymous body, then they walked out and the service began. Louella had half expected Latin and swirls of incense, but it appeared that Caroline had wanted the barest minimum her church provided. The priest's genuine personal regret came through his pastoral duty and Louella had caught several tears on the fingers of purple gloves before everyone left the church and walked to a waiting grave and the painful last moments. As the coffin was slowly lowered, she only had thoughts for more than twenty years of shared friendship; as it finished and she watched the priest shake Ted Owen's hand in sympathy, anger that Caroline was dead flooded back into her. She trembled and felt Maltravers, who was standing next to her, take hold of her arm comfortingly. Tokens of earth fell on hollow wood and Louella wept.

"Come on," Maltravers said gently as it all finished. "They can't bury good memories." Still holding her arm, he led her away from the grave. Jane Root was standing on the path.

"It's a bastard, isn't it?" Her voice was weak with grief. Louella smiled sadly in agreement and the two women embraced each other.

"There's no official wake, but I'm going for a drink with a couple of our authors," Jane told her. "Do you want to come?"

"No, thanks. I think I'd rather be on my own."

"OK. Keep in touch, won't you?"

"Of course I will." Louella looked over Jane's head and saw Ted Owen walking towards the gate, talking to someone she did not know. "I saw you sitting next to Ted in church. I had the idea you'd come together."

"No, it was just chance. This is only the second time I've met him." Jane took her hand. "I really need that drink. I'll call you sometime."

With a faint smile at Maltravers, she turned and walked to where an elderly man was waiting with a young woman and slipped her arm into his. The trio slowly made their way out of the churchyard.

"Good-morning. If you'd like to go back into the church for a few minutes . . ." Trying to speak to all the mourners, the priest had reached them.

Louella looked back at Caroline's grave, waiting for its smothering of dead earth.

"I won't find her there," she replied and swiftly walked away. The priest watched her go unhappily.

"It's all right," Maltravers told him. "She'll appreciate the offer later. It's just that I think she keeps her God somewhere else. Thank you."

He and Tess followed Louella out of the churchyard to where she was standing by her car, fumbling in her bag for keys.

"Let me come with you," Tess suggested. "You really shouldn't be on your own."

"I'm all right." Louella found the keys and unlocked the

door. "I'm going back to the shop and the act will see me through." There was anguish in her face as she looked at Maltravers. "Just find out why they killed her."

He put his arms round her. "I'll try. I want to know as well. We'll be in touch." Louella kissed Tess then got into the car and drove away.

"How are you going to do it?" Tess asked.

"I don't know. All I've got to go on at the moment is that someone's trying to find Jenni Hilton. Perhaps there are some answers there."

Maltravers had somehow expected that Bedford's office would have the traditional seediness of fiction. Instead, the panel in the foyer indicated that the agency was on the third floor, sandwiched between a solicitor and a design company, and he stepped from the lift into a carpeted corridor complete with a well-cared for breadfruit plant in a copper pot next to a door with the agency's name stencilled on mottled glass. A smart receptionist was operating a word-processor in a spotless office and Bedford himself turned out to have the features of a rather kindly judge and the discreet suit of a bank manager.

"I know you said you'd call, but I trust you realise I'm not going to be able to tell you anything," he said, waving Maltravers to a chair. "Unless you can convince me that I've been tricked into doing something illegal, of course."

"I'm not sure about convincing you," Maltravers replied. "But first off, I expect you to keep this conversation as secret as the rest of your business."

"That goes without saying. Discretion is everything in this job."

Bedford's eyes never wavered as he listened; he was obviously absorbing everything. Maltravers restricted himself to essential facts, omitting any suggestion that he suspected Jenni Hilton of murder or any other theories. He could make his point without them.

"And that's it?" Bedford asked finally. "May I make a few comments?"

"Feel free. A new mind might help."

The detective leant forward. "At the bottom line what have

you got? A man died more than twenty years ago, a woman who knew him around that time died last week. There were inquests into both deaths; in one case it was put down as accidental, the other returned an open verdict. You know of nothing to suggest that the police weren't satisfied on either occasion. Right?"

"They questioned Caroline's husband and his girlfriend," Maltravers reminded him. Bedford waved a dismissive hand.

"They checked them out as part of their inquiry and seem to have drawn a blank. It's their job to be suspicious and it proves nothing. Let's get on to what brought you here. You think Jenni Hilton has something to hide because she didn't want this Kershaw mentioned in your interview, but you don't know what it is. I've been asked to discover where she lives and you're suggesting a connection. What is it?"

"If you won't tell me who your client is, I can't know."

"And I've told you I can't reveal that."

"Even if there's something sinister about it? From what I've told you, you've got to admit it's a possibility."

"With enough imagination, anything's possible," Bedford commented. "All I can say is that I'll bear what you've told me in mind and if I have reason to suspect anything, believe me, I'll do something about it. That's my best offer . . . and if you find out anything definite, I'd like to know as well."

"You will," Maltravers assured him. "Incidentally, when we spoke on the phone, you said that your client could be someone chasing a bad debt. That suggests he or she is in business. Is that right, or is this a personal inquiry? Or can't you even say that?"

"Not even that, I'm afraid. And I'm going to have to say that the bad debt comment was nothing more than an example of what it might have been. You picked it up smartly, but don't read anything into it."

Maltravers was dissatisfied, but had no other arguments to offer or any reason to become angry. Bedford clearly ran a respectable operation finding information which people had a right to know. Everything about the man indicated that he was honest.

"All right I've made my point." He stood up. "Somehow I

feel better having met you. I'd have been worried if you'd turned out to be like I expected."

Bedford laughed. "Chandler and Bogart have got a lot to answer for. Between serving court summonses, chasing up people who've disappeared owing money and tracing witnesses for lawyers, this job's about as exciting as market gardening. Can you see yourself out? I'll be in touch if I need to. Believe me."

Maltravers accepted the assurance and left; Bedford opened a drawer in his desk as he heard him say goodbye to the receptionist, stopped the tape recorder and pressed rewind. Had he guessed it was there? Probably, he was nobody's fool and Bedford had been grateful that the conversation had not moved into areas where he would have had to lie; he felt that might have been spotted. He played back the comments about Barry Kershaw, then switched the machine off again.

"What are you up to, Terry?" he murmured to himself. "This isn't just coincidence."

He pulled a pad towards him and began to make notes. Was there any connection with Stephanie? Unlikely, because that had come after the first request to find Jenni Hilton's address. This Barry Kershaw—Terry's brother? cousin? uncle? father even?—had known her, so did Terry just want to meet her for old time's sake? If so, why hadn't he said that? Bedford did not have a rule that he must be told clients' motives, unless he had some reason. In this case, there hadn't been one. Insignia Motors were good customers, Terry was a damn sight more straight than many in that trade. Every job he'd asked to be done in the past had been legitimate, why shouldn't this one be as well?

Bedford felt a vague unease as faint alarm bells grew fractionally louder. When he next reported on Stephanie, he'd raise it and see what the reaction was. But he rather wished Maltravers had been to see him before he had passed on Jenni Hilton's address; knowing what he knew now, he might have pressed Terry Kershaw for some information before doing so.

Maltravers went straight from Bedford's office to *The Chronicle*, less than ten minutes' walk away. As he strolled up to Mike

Fraser's desk, the features editor threw down a manuscript he was reading as though grateful for an excuse to stop.

"I should never have commissioned this clown," he said. "I ask for an assessment of the new Education Bill and he gives me three pars on that, then eight hundred words of his memories of Winchester and how public schools make a man of you. Prat."

"A drink will make you feel better," Maltravers told him. "And I want to bounce some ideas off you and see what you think."

Fraser looked at him sharply. "Sounds serious for a Monday morning."

"Perhaps you'll persuade me I'm over-reacting."

They went to the Volunteer again, almost empty with more than an hour to go before most people's lunch breaks and sat on high stools against a shelf running under the windows. Maltravers had started to explain as they crossed the graveyard, and when they had collected their drinks, Fraser sat in complete silence while he listened to the rest.

"They teach you to keep quiet in the Samaritans, I assume," Maltravers commented when he finished. "There were a dozen times when a journalist would have wanted to ask questions."

"I suddenly find I'm wearing both hats," Fraser replied. "This is worrying you, isn't it?"

"A lot." Maltravers sighed and contemplated the beer remaining in his glass. "Bedford's straight enough. I can't complain about how he found me, but . . . has anyone been in touch with the office asking where Jenni Hilton lives?"

"Not as far as I know. The only thing we could have done was invite them to write to us and we'd pass the letter on."

"Then why didn't whoever's hired Bedford do that if they just wanted to contact her? If it was someone she didn't want to know, she could have ignored the letter of course. So who *needs* to know where she is? And why?"

"It looks devious," Fraser agreed. "Have you told her about this? You ought to."

"I can't at the moment. She told me she was going away the weekend the piece appeared to see her son in Exeter. She's due back the day after tomorrow."

"Then you can assume that she's safe enough there," Fraser

commented. "There's also no guarantee that this Bedford character will manage to find the address and pass it on."

"I'm not counting on that. Even in London, if someone's looking hard enough they'll find you eventually. Jenni Hilton isn't a hermit but her movements will be within a limited area. Bedford's quite capable of working that out. It's only a matter of time."

"Well, you can leave it lie for a couple of days," Fraser pointed out. "As long as she's out of town, she can't be in any danger, even if someone finds her address . . . And is she really in any danger?"

"Until I know otherwise, she could be."

Fraser grimaced in agreement. "As I see it, the only person you know of who could be mixed up somehow is this Ted Owen. Why not face him with it? If he's not involved, there's nothing lost and if he is but denies it at least he'll know you're suspicious."

Maltravers looked dubious as he tapped his own chest. "This is not the stuff of which *Boys' Own* heroes are made. I have no wish to end up down a dark alley with my head bashed in."

"Bit over-dramatic," Fraser commented.

"Maybe. But everybody who knew Barry Kershaw is convinced he was murdered. I've got a theory that Jenni Hilton did it, but for all I know it might have been Ted Owen. There could have been a connection between him and Kershaw that I haven't found yet. However, I'm as positive as I can be that he was involved in killing his wife. He could be making a habit of it. Perhaps murder's like adultery—it's easier after the first time."

"You speak from experience?"

"Only of adultery."

Chapter Fifteen

"Minister, the question many people—including some backbenchers in your own party—are asking is how the Government can propose what they see as cuts in the money available to state schools, while at the same time increasing the tax benefits that public schools enjoy. Labour says this is hurting ordinary people at the expense of the privileged. What do you have to say to these criticisms?"

The politician granted the television interviewer a smile that combined resigned acceptance that such a question should be asked with a faintly sympathetic amazement that any creature able to walk upright could be unable to see the unarguable wisdom of Government policy.

"The first point of course is that there are no cuts," he said smoothly. "Let that be clearly understood. The White Paper talks of rationalisation, a determination to get better value for money. With regard to the public schools policy, you must completely separate the issues here. It's very important not to confuse the two, they're nothing to do with each other. Britain's public schools are, and have been for many years, centres of excellence. Not the only ones of course—many of our state schools maintain the highest standards—but private education makes an enormous contribution. The Labour party has always refused to recognise this, and when their spokesman says that . . ."

Maltravers yawned as the glib response moved away from the question and into political sniping. Told what to say by ingenious civil servants, advised on how to dress, gesture, even comb their hair by experts on personal presentation, senior politicians knew exactly how to appear totally reasonable while defending any policy, however ludicrous or dictated by party prejudice. All sides were as good—or as bad—as the others at doing it. He had turned on *Newsnight* for another item on Monday evening and was too idle either to turn the set off or even get up and press the mute button on the remote control as he waited for the following programme on Iris Murdoch. As he stared at the screen without taking very much in, Jenni Hilton, Barry Kershaw, Louella Sinclair, Caroline Owen, Jack Buxton, Ted Owen and Daphne Gillie, even Alan Bedford, floated about his mind, tangled and inviting theories. Suppose that . . . No, that makes no sense. How about . . . but that can't be true, because if it were then . . .

"How bloody *stupid*!"

Engrossed in an entertaining but questionably accurate piece in *Private Eye*, Tess jumped as he shouted, then her attention switched to the television screen.

". . . so it is for schools that opt out of local authority control to decide how best to spend their resources. The Government will merely provide a framework, we will *not* tell them what they should do. And that sort of freedom is exactly what Labour would deny them if . . ."

"You don't usually get so excited," she remarked mildly. "What did he say that was especially idiotic?"

"He actually said something that made sense . . . No, I don't mean that, I've hardly been listening." Maltravers was sitting up in his chair, suddenly animated. "He said that two things—whatever they were—had to be kept separate, that they shouldn't be confused with each other. That's it."

"That's what?" Tess asked uncertainly.

Maltravers replied rather slowly, thinking through ramifications as he spoke. "We've got to separate Kershaw's death from Caroline's. Look at them as though they're absolutely unconnected."

"But we've always thought that . . ."

"Precisely," he interrupted. "Because they knew each other and because both their deaths were suspicious, we automatically jumped to the conclusion that there was a connection and may have been completely wasting time looking for it. But . . . think of it this way. Assume that I and any one of—I don't know—

probably twenty-odd other journalists in London was murdered tomorrow. If the police traced our careers back far enough, they'd find we worked together at some point. But that wouldn't mean our deaths had anything in common. We knew each other years ago, but after that our lives had gone their different ways. You see what I'm getting at?"

Tess nodded. "Yes, I do. Louella said she'd been able to trace hardly any of the crowd from the Sixties. They're scattered all over the place. They've lost touch."

"But Caroline had stayed in London—and kept in touch with Louella," said Maltravers. "Because *that* link from the Sixties had remained in place, we've been hung up on the idea that there had to be another connecting Kershaw's and Caroline's deaths. So kick that into touch and start again."

"Right." Instantly grasping the situation, Tess's mind was working as fast as his. "Barry Kershaw was almost certainly murdered, but that's nothing to do with Caroline's death . . . So was she murdered? Or is the accident theory right?"

"Possibly," he acknowledged, "but there were doubts about it. The police thought it was worth checking and discovered that Daphne Gillie was near Tottenham Court Road station at the wrong time. But there was no motive they could see and they dropped it. What else is there?"

"There's the engagement of course," Tess reminded him. "None of us can understand why that's happened so quickly—and the marriage is suddenly being arranged in a hurry. Is that relevant?"

Maltravers stood up and began to pace, adrenalising his brain with physical movement. "It's certainly inexplicable. Before Caroline died, they were prepared to wait, suddenly they go into overdrive . . . just a minute! There was something that Jane Root told me. She once heard part of a phone conversation between Caroline and Ted. She was saying she wouldn't go along with a divorce, and . . . What the hell was it? I questioned Jane about it at the time, because—That's it. Caroline said something about not caring how much money was involved."

"You never mentioned this," Tess said.

"It didn't seem relevant when we were running around looking for connections with Barry Kershaw. It turned out there was no hassle over money involving Caroline and Ted. Everything had been settled when they split up and Scimitar Press is hardly worth a fortune. He'll get about twenty thousand pounds top weight when it's sold. At his sort of income level, that's not worth falling out over, let alone killing for . . . so Caroline must have been talking about some other money. So what was it?"

"Whatever it was, it seems to be tied up with the divorce," Tess observed. "Did they own a house, which . . .?"

"No." Frustration that they might be on to something they could not see made Maltravers snap with impatience. "They'd sold the house when they separated and shared out the money. They'd done everything to end the marriage except sign on the dotted line."

"But the conversation Jane overheard was still about the divorce," Tess insisted. "There's no need to stamp on my suggestions."

"Sorry." Maltravers gave her an absent kiss of apology as he sat on the settee again. "Let's do this calmly. One, Ted Owen would only get excited about money with a lot of noughts attached. Two, that sort of money was somehow linked with his being married to Caroline. Three . . ."

"Wrong," Tess corrected. "It was linked with his being *divorced* from Caroline . . . but you say the divorce wouldn't bring him anything. Or at least not enough to get him excited."

Maltravers grunted in agreement as the separated-out question of Caroline Owen's death produced its own inexplicable facets.

"There was something else Jane said, but I can't quite remember . . ." He shook his head in irritation. "When Caroline put the phone down she made some comment about . . . What was it? That's it! Sod her bloody aunt!"

"Sod whose bloody aunt?" Tess demanded.

"Daphne's presumably . . . but where does it get us?"

"Does she have an aunt? Didn't Louella say her parents died in a road crash when she was a teenager?"

"Yes . . . and she was brought up by someone else. The aunt?"

"Perhaps . . . but where does money come into it?"

"Think it through," Maltravers said. "We may be getting somewhere. There's a relation—an aunt—and there's money. Tie them together."

"Rich aunt?" Tess asked.

"Very possibly . . . and one who doesn't approve of her niece living in sin?" Maltravers suggested. "The sort who'd cut her out of her will unless she got married?"

"But what's the big hurry? Unless auntie's about to peg out."

"And if auntie's worth a packet, it could be a motive for murder." Maltravers stood up. "I'm going to phone Louella. Caroline may have said something to her."

Tess was still turning it round in her mind when he came back into the room five minutes later. He looked disappointed.

"As far as Louella knows Daphne's only living relative is a brother. And the two of them were brought up by their godparents. Ted was apparently quite open with Caroline about her. So no dying aunt."

"But there's still an aunt somewhere," Tess commented. "Alive or dead."

"And if not alive, then certainly dead." Maltravers looked at her for a moment and she saw confused realisation cross his face. "So does that bring us back to a will?"

"Can't fault it, but explain."

"If I could explain, I wouldn't be fumbling around."

Tess crossed to the drinks trolley. "Stimulation," she said as she returned with two tumblers. "We need it."

"Thanks." Maltravers accepted the glass. "Let's go back to Daphne's parents for a moment. She was only a teenager when they died, so any money they left could have gone into some sort of trust until she reached a certain age."

"Then she's probably got it now," Tess pointed out. "She's nearly twenty-five isn't she?"

"Yes, but we don't know anything about her parents. They could have specified any age . . . All right, not any age, but older than twenty-one."

"So? Whatever it was, if she lives long enough she gets it. And what's it got to do with this aunt?"

"Same principle. She's also apparently dead, so the money Ted and Caroline were arguing about must be locked up in a will. If we could find that will it might tell us something."

"How do we do that? We don't even know who she is . . . or did Caroline tell Louella?"

"No. The only possibility is to look at her parents' wills and see if there's anything in them."

"Same problem," Tess objected. "How do you find them?"

"Wills are public documents and anyone can go to Somerset House and look at anybody else's. Believe it or not, there's an agency rejoicing in the name of Smee and Ford which makes a living selling the details to local newspapers. People often get cross about them being published, but there's nothing they can do to stop it."

"All right, but how do you find them?"

"We have a name—and Gillie's fairly unusual fortunately—and they died about ten years ago. I've never been to Somerset House, but they must have a cataloguing system. I'll call David Shirley my solicitor in the morning and ask him how it works."

Tess looked dubious. "It's a long shot. Even if you find her parents' wills, they might not tell you anything."

"It's all we've got at the moment . . . and of course if her aunt was also a Gillie, I might be able to find her will as well. Now that could be interesting."

"I bet she married someone called Smith."

"Pessimist. Anyway, it's somewhere to start and fits in with what little we know."

"It's faintly weird, but worth looking into," Tess agreed. "But where does it leave you with Kershaw and Jenni Hilton?"

"I'm positive there's a link there and it may be easier to sort out if we can remove Caroline's death from the picture," Maltravers replied. "The immediate question is why is somebody trying to find her address? I don't like that, but we don't have to worry about it until she gets back to London in a couple of days. Then I'll call her . . . and see if I can persuade her to talk about it. If necessary, I'll tell her what I know about her affair with Jack Buxton."

"Are you going to put forward your theory that that gave her a motive to kill Kershaw?"

"If I have to, yes. Not because it particularly bothers me, but because if it's true, then whoever's trying to find her could be big trouble."

"Somebody who knows something and is going to blackmail her?" Tess suggested.

"I wish I could believe that, but all they'd have needed to do was write to her through *The Chronicle*. That would keep them anonymous as well." Maltravers swirled his drink and watched dissolving ice cubes spin. "Trying to find where she lives must mean that someone wants to go there. I can think of only one reason why anyone should want that. Someone else suspects—perhaps even knows—that she killed Kershaw . . . and they could want revenge."

"After all these years?" Tess raised her hand, gesturing away something outrageous. "Darling, come on. That's too much."

"You have other ideas for the committee to consider?"

"Not off the top of my head, but who could it be? Louella said that everyone hated Kershaw and was glad he was dead."

"But his family weren't," he reminded her. "Don't you remember Louella telling us what a row his mother made at the inquest?"

"Well, she must be pushing it now, even if she's still alive," Tess argued.

"Another relative then, or perhaps some friend from the East End who wasn't part of his glamorous life. If he was as big a villain as we've been told, he could have been tied up with the Kray twins and their gang for all we know. He certainly knew where to hire those thugs who worked Jack Buxton over. Until we find out—if we ever do—who's asked a private detective to trace Jenni Hilton, then I think we must assume the worst. At least I'll be able to warn her when she gets back to town."

"What about tracing his family?" Tess suggested.

"How?" Maltravers demanded. "He came from Wapping didn't he? From Tower Bridge down river, London's been torn up and started over again. The street Kershaw was born in probably isn't there any more, let alone have his family still living in it. And suppose I did find them, what could I do? Knock on the door and say, 'Hey, is one of you planning to murder Jenni Hilton?' If I'm wrong they thump me, if I'm right, the river police are fishing me out of the Thames. I can't swim even without a hundredweight of concrete tied to my ankles."

"Would it help to tell the police all this now?" Tess suggested.

"What's to tell? Put all the pieces together and it still doesn't add up to much. Louella's convinced Barry Kershaw was murdered, I suspect there's something behind Jenni Hilton not wanting his name mentioned in a feature about her, Alan Bedford's been asked to find her address for someone. They're hardly going to put an armed guard outside her house on the strength of that lot. More likely they'd start talking to some of the people who lied at Kershaw's inquest and begin pressing perjury charges, if they're still allowed to do so after all this time."

"So what can you do?"

"Check out our theory about Daphne Gillie. Warn Jenni when she gets back. Perhaps see Bedford again and convince him he could be helping somebody to commit murder . . . and pray?" He grinned sourly.

"Do agnostics believe in prayer?"

"This one does. I also believe they're answered—but not always the way we expect them to be."

Alan Bedford rang Insignia Motors on Tuesday morning and made an appointment to see Terry Kershaw at eleven o'clock. He could have given him the information he had over the phone, but wanted to see him personally when he asked certain questions. Maltravers had planted enough doubts in his mind to cause him concern. When he arrived, Kershaw was looking as though he had slept badly.

"What have you got?" he asked wearily as the secretary closed the door behind her.

Bedford took a notebook from his briefcase. "Stephanie left your house shortly after nine yesterday morning. She went to a shop in Highgate village where she apparently bought shoes and then drove to Mill Hill and parked outside number forty-three Fawcett Avenue. She was seen to enter the house and remained there until four o'clock before returning home. My girl checked the electoral roll at the local library and the resident was given as . . ."

"I know," Kershaw's voice was dead as he interrupted. "He's one of our salesmen. Rang in yesterday and said he was ill. It's happened a couple of times lately."

"I see." Kershaw closed his notebook. "Do you want me to continue having her followed?"

"No thanks. I don't want to know any more. I'll take it from here."

"What I've told you isn't much use in any legal action," Bedford pointed out. "For all I know she was visiting the sick. She could deny there was anything more to it than that. If you're thinking of starting proceedings, you'll need more. Just reminding you."

"I realise that. I'll deal with it my way. Thanks Alan."

Kershaw turned round in his swivel chair and looked out of the window. In other circumstances, Bedford would have taken it as a sign that he just wanted to be left alone.

"There's something else I want to talk to you about, Terry," he said.

"What?" Kershaw sounded preoccupied and indifferent as he remained with his back to him.

"This Jenni Hilton inquiry you asked me to make . . ." Bedford registered the twitch of tension in the slight movement of Kershaw's head. "Somebody's been to see me about it and I'm concerned."

"Concerned?" Kershaw turned to face him again. "What about?"

"I've been told that she knew someone called Barry Kershaw years ago. He's dead now. Relative of yours?"

"My brother."

"You didn't mention that."

Kershaw shrugged. "Does it matter? I saw no need to tell you the family history . . . Who came to see you about this?"

"I can't say. You know that."

"So what did whoever it was say that's worrying you?"

"Enough."

"That's no answer."

"It's all I'm saying at this stage," Bedford told him. "I just want it putting on the record that if I discover anything that makes me—let's say have doubts about your motives—I may have to do something about it to protect my firm's reputation."

"Have I ever been less than straight with you in the past?"

"No. And that's what I don't like about this."

For a few moments the only sound was the muffled rumble of the North Circular Road, then Kershaw said, "There's nothing to worry about, Alan. I've not asked you to do anything wrong."

"I know that. But I don't know why you've asked me and I'd feel happier if I did."

"What you don't know can't hurt you." Kershaw smiled sourly. "That's what my mum always used to tell me. Forget it."

Bedford waited, but there was obviously no more coming as Kershaw looked at him impassively. He slipped the notebook back in his briefcase and left. In his car he repeated the entire conversation, virtually word for word, into a tape recorder then sat for a few minutes, fingers of his right hand making rapid four-stroke drumbeats on the steering wheel. Terry Kershaw had never been a good liar—incredible, considering that he had started in the second-hand car trade—and he was lying now. Bedford was becoming increasingly convinced that he should talk to Augustus Maltravers again.

Kershaw was shaken out of his thoughts by his secretary calling him on the intercom.

"The gentlemen from Honda are here, Mr Kershaw. Shall I bring them through?"

"Can you ask them to wait for a moment, Judy? Make them coffee."

He flicked the intercom button off and picked up his private line telephone.

"Hello, Mum. I've found that address for you."

Not for her. Not for Barry. Not for any reason he could explain. Perhaps for Stephanie. To hurt her as well, to hit back like an angry child.

Chapter Sixteen

Surrounded by façades of decorated Portland stone, Maltravers crossed the square quadrangle of Somerset House from the gates off the Strand and went through the double doors in the south wing with PRINCIPAL REGISTRY OF THE FAMILY DIVISION in gold lettering above them. Beneath his feet, somewhere in eleven miles of corridors, was kept a copy of every will which had been through probate in England and Wales since 1858. Had he wished, he could have read any one of them; only those of the Royal family remain private. Even Karl Marx felt it necessary to write a will rather than simply bequeathing everything to the toiling masses, and a soldier once simply put "I leave everything to her" on the back of an envelope. It is the shortest will among millions, although probate was never granted, possibly because of the problem of deciding who he was referring to.

Immediately inside the doors, the entrance hall was lined with hundreds of bound calendar books, immense alphabetical-order volumes bound in dark red leather, marked with the years. Inside each one were basic details of names, addresses and when probate was granted. It was only just turned eleven o'clock, but there were already thirty or so people pulling them off the shelves and poring over their entries; solicitors' clerks checking recondite conditions of final wishes, people tracing family history, the hopeful looking for some legacy to which they were convinced they were entitled. The appropriate entry located, they took the books to a desk near the window overlooking the Thames and the details were written on a form which was slipped through a slot in the wall. Within half an hour, they would hear the name called and could see the copy in question for twenty-five pence; if it was what they wanted, they could have their own copy sent to them for another twenty-five pence a page.

Maltravers spent a few moments observing the system in operation, then found the stretch of books for 1980 which seemed a reasonable year to start. As well as the surname, he also knew Daphne's parents had lived in Dorset. There was nothing for anyone called Gillie in that year, so he moved back along the shelf and looked in 1979. Bernard William Gillie's will had been through probate on December fourteenth and he lived in Dorchester; immediately below that entry was one for Marion Ruth Gillie. Maltravers carried the volume to the desk and his request for both wills went through. He spent the next twenty minutes idly looking up entries for well-known people whose dates of death he could remember, discovering that Charles Dickens had left some eighty thousand pounds in 1870. He was still trying to calculate how much that would have made him worth in modern terms when "Gillie!" rang across the room. He went to the desk, was sent along the corridor to first pay his fifty pence to the cashier, and returned to collect the copies.

The wills were initially complementary, each leaving everything to the other before they dealt with the question of predecease. Here there were slight variations, but the main parts were the same. The entire estate was left to their son Martin David Gillie and Daphne Elizabeth Gillie was to receive one thousand pounds a year until she reached the age of twenty-five. The phraseology after that was identical: "The legacy to my daughter takes into account the monies she is due to receive at that age under the terms of the will of Constance Elizabeth Gillie."

"Hello, Constance. Are you auntie?" Maltravers murmured to himself. He reached into his pocket for a pen, then remembered something he had half noticed earlier. Turning round he saw the signs saying that brief notes could only be taken in pencil and everybody appeared to be observing it. He searched his pockets unsuccessfully. "Dammit."

He was directed to one of the messengers who led him to a

desk where a collection of pencil stubs, none more than three inches long, was kept.

"Do they steal them if you hand out long ones?" he asked.

"That's it," the messenger said cheerfully. "We've got full ones, but they always disappear."

"I shall faithfully return it," Maltravers promised and went back to his table. He copied out the key passages, handed the wills back, then returned to the shelves and started working backwards, looking for Constance Elizabeth. At least the surname was the rare Gillie again, but this time he had no idea of the year. The efficiency of the system was such that it only took him a few minutes to find her in 1975 and he went through the ordering process again. While he was waiting, he reread the brief calendar book entry and noticed that her address was given as Prestbury in Cheshire, some twenty miles from where he had been born and brought up. While the poor were always with mankind, they did not live in Prestbury, which had been one of the most exclusive villages in Britain in his childhood and still was as far as he knew. Constance Elizabeth had had money. Her will, when he received it, did not say how much, but he could make an educated guess. There were a handful of minor bequests, then came the critical paragraphs.

4. I leave to my nephew, Bernard William Gillie of Dorchester in the County of Dorset, the sum of £10,000 and a similar sum to his wife, Marion Ruth Gillie, in recognition of their many kindnesses to me. To my great-nephew, Martin David Gillie, a minor, I bequeath the sum of £5,000 to be held in trust until he reaches the age of twenty-one years.

5. The residue of my estate, I leave to my great-niece Daphne Elizabeth Gillie, a minor, also of Dorchester in the County of Dorset, to be held in trust until she attains the age of twenty-five years, provided and absolutely that she is a married woman and living with her legal spouse at that time. I hereby appoint Messrs Goode and Wilson, solicitors, of Macclesfield in the County of Cheshire, trustees of these monies, together with all sums realised by the sale of property, goods, chattels and all and any other appurtenances, to be invested taking best advice as and when the occasion may arise according to their best

judgement until Daphne Elizabeth Gillie shall be of age under the terms of this Will and fulfil the obligations herein.
6. Should my said great-niece, Daphne Elizabeth Gillie, fail to fulfil absolutely the terms above, any and all monies are to be distributed to the following charitable causes . . .

Maltravers sighed with satisfaction and a certain disbelief. He had been prepared to draw a blank; discovering how right he was surprised him. But how much was involved? Constance had handed down twenty-five thousand pounds to three relatives and nearly another five thousand pounds in minor bequests; what had that left for Daphne? He copied out the vital paragraphs and returned the will to the desk where he asked if it was possible to discover how much someone's estate was worth. It would need an initial inquiry to the solicitors who had drawn up the document and then an approach to the Inland Revenue. There should be no difficulty; like the wills themselves, such information was a matter of public record.

Back in the Strand, Maltravers walked towards Trafalgar Square and took his thoughts into a Pizza Hut for lunch. He doubted that a solicitor would open his heart to a stranger who strolled in with a murder theory and going through the tangles of official channels would take time. It was obviously possible that the police would take action on what he could already tell them, but it would be satisfying to be able to present them with as full a story as possible. Perhaps . . . he glanced at his watch. His own solicitor would probably be at lunch himself. He could try later. As he ate his lasagne, self-satisfaction was deflated by the knowledge that separating Caroline Owen's death from that of Barry Kershaw may have been inspired, but still left the question of who had asked Alan Bedford for Jenni Hilton's address unanswered. And that, he was convinced, was more serious.

Tess spent Tuesday morning in an echoing, cavernous hall which had eventually had its direct line to God cut off, because of a marked decline among Baptists in Paddington, and was now used as a meeting place for the area's Asian community. It had been hired by the director of a new stage adaptation of Mrs

Henry Wood's *East Lynne*, a book which Tess had found hilariously readable, and she relished playing it in serious high-camp style. She was auditioning for the part of Lady Isabel, whose little personal problems reach their climax when she returns home to become resident nanny to her own children, so altered by life's vicissitudes that neither they nor her remarried husband, who thinks she is dead, recognise her. In the best traditions of nineteenth-century melodrama, one of the children is marked to die and duly does.

"Dead!" Tess's agonised scream sang round high walls of grubby green paint. "Dead! And never called me mother!" Victorian anguish in black leggings and Indian cotton smock, she flamboyantly raised her hand, pressed the back of her wrist against her forehead, and fainted.

"Very good!" The producer smiled from the back of the hall as she sat up and looked at him inquiringly. "Can you give it some more over-the-top spin? All the stops out."

"If that's what you want." Tess stood up and brushed dust off with her hand. She flicked back through the script she was holding and turned to the other two actors, playing the scene with her, who had already been cast. "From the start of page a hundred and forty-three? I'll collapse on my knees earlier this time."

By lunchtime they were becoming slightly insane, adding lines of their own as they tried to make the preposterous even more outrageous. Tess finally delivered her immortal remark in a tripe-thick Lancashire accent and rolled about the stage, drumming her heels in hysterics as they all cracked up.

"And there's trouble at t'mill, an' all!" she choked out. "Ee, life's a real bugger at times, innit?"

She dropped her script and wiped away tears and she sat up, weak with laughter. "If I get this, don't anyone bloody dare say that to me before I go on. Gavin, that's it. I can't do it again at the moment."

"No need to, darling," the producer told her. "All you had to do was convince me you could play melodrama and you've done it. What's your availability?"

"I've got a couple of days dubbing with London Weekend at

the end of the month and a short-story recording for the Beeb," she told him. "Apart from that, I'm clear."

"Fine. I'll call your agent and fix the contract."

"Thank you." Tess sighed, half with satisfaction, half with alarm at what she had done. "Remember what Larry Olivier said about acting? It's no profession for adults. God, what have I let myself in for?"

"A super part. Don't knock it. See you at rehearsals."

Tess would have liked a drink, but everyone had other engagements and she wandered down to Bayswater Road wondering what to do. Maltravers had said he expected to be out most of the day. On impulse she hailed a taxi and went to Syllabub, deciding to treat herself to a celebration. The shop was empty and Louella Sinclair sent one of her assistants out to buy fruit and cheese which she and Tess shared in the back room.

"How's Gus getting on?" Louella asked. Maltravers had called her a second time the previous evening to explain what he had worked out.

"Digging through musty wills at Somerset House." Tess helped herself to smoked Austrian. "I'm not convinced he'll turn up anything, but I've got to agree that his theory makes sense."

Louella suddenly looked very unhappy. "If he's right, it means Caroline was killed because someone wants even more money than they've got already. That's disgusting."

"I know," Tess agreed sympathetically. "Gus was quoting from a Father Brown story last night. Something like, 'If he's clever enough to make so much money, then he must be stupid enough to want it.'"

"He?" Louella queried. "It's possible that Ted doesn't know what happened. Daphne could have acted on her own."

Tess shook her head. "Gus suggested that, but I don't know that I can go along with it. If Daphne did do it without telling him, he'd suspect her more than anyone else. Hardly a basis for a marriage."

"That depends what sort of basis you want," Louella said. "This one will be based on Daphne's desire to claw her way to the top in the advertising business, Ted's conceit at pulling a girl young enough to be his daughter—classic middle-age fantasy—and both of them being very rich. I know that's cynical—but I think it's true."

"Then let's just hope that Gus is right and he can prove it. That'll take the gloss off."

"Will it? I'm not sure."

"What do you mean?"

"Think it through," Louella told her. "I have. Even if Gus finds some money somewhere that depended on Caroline's death, how can he—or anyone else—prove that Daphne actually murdered her? She could just go on denying it."

"Yes, but both she and Ted told the police there was no panic about getting married," Tess argued. "If there is, because it would mean she would inherit money, it means they lied—or at least she did. The police are going to lean on them like crazy."

"Lean certainly," Louella agreed. "But break? Don't count on it. Whether Ted planned it with Daphne or she's kept him in the dark, they could both just deny it and challenge the police to come up with some proof. If it came to a court case, Ted could afford the best QC there is. All there'd be would be suspicion."

"Hell of a lot of it."

"Yes, but that could be all. A good lawyer could knock down any prosecution case based on that."

Tess squeezed crumbs of cheese together on the plate with her fingers, thinking as she ate them. "So you believe that even if Gus turns up everything he's hoping for, Ted and Daphne could still brazen it out and get away with it?"

"I'm certain they'll brazen it out—and, yes, I think they'll get away with it."

"How do you feel about that?"

Louella's mouth twitched with distaste. "Resentful, I expect. But nothing's going to bring Caroline back . . . and I'm in no position to get on my high horse about justice. Don't forget that I've been at least some sort of accessory to murder. I could have told the police that Barry Kershaw never took drugs. But I didn't."

"That was rather different. He deserved it, Caroline didn't."

"I don't think the law would look at it like that," Louella said. "And do you? Who else doesn't deserve to live, Tess?"

Maureen Kershaw gloated over her A-Z Street Atlas of London, a thick circle drawn with a ballpoint pen around Cheyne Street, a bright red fence through which Jenni Hilton could not pass. Her first instinct had been to go there immediately, but then she had stopped herself. Think it through again. Sleep on it. Savour the taste of it, the anticipation that it was finally going to happen after all these years. The bag was just the right size to hide the bayonet, she had worked out exactly how to get there. Take a taxi into town—not to Cheyne Street of course, the driver might remember her. Then the Underground to Sloane Square; that seemed the nearest station. Walk down the King's Road where Barry had sometimes taken her. She had memorised the map completely. The eighth turning on the left was Flood Street; down there and then right. Not a long street, not many houses. The sort of area where neighbours kept themselves to themselves, didn't peer out of windows minding other people's business. Not taking any notice of a woman walking past on her own, probably not even seeing her. They wouldn't see her leave either. Within minutes she could be on the Embankment near the Royal Hospital where the Chelsea Pensioners lived. She might have to risk another taxi then to get away from the area quickly; they'd be busy and he wouldn't remember her. Get out somewhere near the station, catch a train home. Barry would be proud of his mum working it all out. Barry had always been proud of her. She turned pages in one of the photograph albums, frozen images already looking old-fashioned, of the time when she had been happy. She would never really be happy again, but at least she would be content that she had done right by her favourite boy.

Terry Kershaw had certainly not expected contrition, but he had been prepared for denial; he received amused contempt and resentment.

"I don't interfere with your private life, just stay out of mine," Stephanie told him. "If I want to make friends, I'll do so."

"We're not talking about friends. We're talking about spending the day with a man. In his house. You weren't there just for coffee."

"Actually we did have coffee." She taunted him with eyes of hungry recollection. "Before and afterwards."

"You bloody cow! I've never given you any reason for this."

"Oh, yes you have. You're doing it now. Why don't you hit me? Go on."

She stood right in front of him, inviting and challenging, and pointed to her face. "Right there! Have the goddamed guts to hit me where it will show."

Inflamed, he raised his hand then dropped it and turned away, defeated by the defiance in her face. All the Kershaw violence had been given to Barry.

"Can't you see?" she demanded. "I told you before we married I needed a strong man like my father. At the time I thought I was getting one, but you're only strong at the office, not here where I need it. You've let me down so many times."

"And your toy-boy doesn't of course." A sense of self-contempt, of not being able to do what he knew he should, drove him to fight on with sarcasm. "He's playing with you, you know. Getting a kick out of laying the boss's wife."

"Do you think I don't know that? I'm playing with him as well. It amuses me." She turned away indifferently. "I always quit while I'm ahead."

Kershaw felt a deadening shock as the truth of a suspicion he had been pushing away was casually hurled at him. "He's not the first?"

"The first?" she mocked. "You don't understand anything, do you? I've been screwing around for the past five years. Do you want the full list? It began with . . ."

"Shut up!" He grabbed her shoulder and for one moment she really thought he was going to hit her, but he let go as though frightened at what she was driving him to. "I don't want to know. Let's just start divorce proceedings and get it over with."

"Divorce? No way, Terry. You start that and I'll tell Daddy you've been flaunting your girlfriends at me. I'll say you've been spending your money on them instead of me and the twins."

He stared at her in disbelief. "You lying bitch!"

"I know that, you know that. Daddy will listen to me. He always does. You'll be out of Insignia Motors so fast you won't believe it. And I'll make sure the best you'll get will be selling second-hand wrecks in . . . I don't know . . . the bloody East End where you come from." Her face changed from threats to a sudden realisation. "You can go and live with your mum again, can't you? I never got you out of there, so you might as well go back."

He was unable to comprehend. "You want this to go on? What for?"

"Because it suits me. Because I don't want the mess of us splitting up at the moment. It would upset the girls. Don't worry, we'll probably do it eventually. In the meantime we put on the act, right? Plenty of other people do." She gave a fast, impatient sigh of annoyance at the reaction she saw in his face. "Stop being so . . . so working class! You always said you wanted to put that behind you. Use a bit of the sophistication you were so anxious to learn. You fought your way into this lifestyle, now start living it!"

She glared, then turned her back on him and started to walk out of the room. "Make the best of it, Terry."

The door closed and he heard her calling their daughters' names, asking what they were doing as though everything was completely normal in their home. He remembered a woman when he was a teenager who had been caught having an affair—not that phrase in the East End, of course; she "had a fancy man"—and her husband found out. He belted her half-senseless and sorted out the boyfriend before getting drunk. After that the marriage had continued, the wife defeated, but in some perverse way respecting him. That had been Etruria Street's way of handling the situation; apart from the violence, was it all that different from how such matters were arranged in Highgate? The end result was the same—no divorce and the pretence remained intact. Terry Kershaw could not hit his wife, so that solution was impossible. Could he accept hypocritical social convention instead? He wasn't sure—he wasn't sure of a lot of things any more. Certainly not his motives in yielding to his mother's demands to be told where Jenni Hilton lived. It was just another failure to defy the first woman who had controlled his life.

Chapter Seventeen

When Maltravers returned to Coppersmith Street on Tuesday afternoon, there was another phone message from Alan Bedford.

"I'd like to talk to you again about this Jenni Hilton business," he said after introducing himself. "I can't explain on the phone, but I'm not very happy about the situation. I'm out for the rest of the day, but I'll be in tomorrow morning if you're free. I think it's better we talk at the office if that's possible. I'll expect you unless you call my secretary and say you can't make it. Goodbye."

"And what have you found out, I wonder?" Maltravers murmured. There was no indication that Bedford was prepared to be any more forthcoming over the identity of his client, but he would not waste time for an idle chat. It was vaguely worrying but, with Jenni Hilton still in Exeter, there was no reason to imagine that anything dangerous was about to happen. Maltravers rang his solicitor to pursue the other half of the problem.

"David, it's Gus. Odd request time. I assume lawyers talk to each other fairly freely and I'd like you to try and find out how much someone's estate was worth."

"Think you've been cheated out of a fortune?"

"Nothing like that, I'm afraid. I forgot to ask for rich relations when I was born. It's someone called Constance Elizabeth Gillie who died in . . ." He explained the background without going into unnecessary details. "If you call these Goode and Wilson people in Macclesfield, is there a chance they'll tell you how much she actually left?"

"It's possible," Shirley acknowledged. "If they can't or won't, we could always chase it through the Inland Revenue."

"I was told that at Somerset House, but I'm trying to short circuit the system."

"What's the big hurry?"

"It's too complicated to explain. Can you have a go at it?"

"Well, you've certainly got me fascinated. I'll call you back."

"Thanks . . . and don't charge me a fortune. I'm broke."

"I might settle for a decent lunch and the full story. You're at home? OK, it shouldn't take long."

As Maltravers rang off, he heard Tess opening the front door. She was singing 'I'm Still Here' from *Follies*.

"I take it that the career is still surviving," he said as she appeared in the doorway. "You got it?"

"Yes, and it's going to be a lulu." She grinned with delight. "I want to go to Highgate Cemetery and put flowers on Mrs Henry Wood's grave for luck."

"You won't need luck," Maltravers assured her. "Come here, my clever girl." They hugged each other and he kissed her on the forehead. "When do rehearsals begin?"

"Couple of weeks. We open the second week in September at the Aldwych. I could still be in work at Christmas."

"And New Year I trust. Celebration dinner somewhere nice I think. How about Bibendum?"

"Marvellous, but it's cheaper at lunchtime."

"Don't worry about it. I'm always ready to spend your money."

"So I've noticed," she said drily. "You're nearly as good at it as I am at spending yours . . . Anyway, how did you get on?"

"Oh, I hit pay dirt as well," Maltravers said feelingly. "We were dead right."

"Daphne was really left money? How much?"

"I'm trying to find that out, but I'm positive it wasn't peanuts. Let's make a cup of tea and I'll tell you."

Tess listened in fascination as he told her the story, quoting from the key passages of the wills.

"Good God," she said. "I thought I'd had my share of the preposterous at Paddington. Why on earth did this Constance woman include a condition like that?"

"I don't know, but perhaps David will turn up something on that as well as just how much is involved." The phone rang in the front room. "And that could be him calling back."

Tess was left frustrated for nearly ten minutes before Maltravers returned.

"Chapter and verse." He tapped a sheet of paper he was holding. "David found he was talking to a solicitor he met at some Law Society dinner who actually drew up Constance's will and remembers her very well. Her fiancé was killed in the First World War and she never married. Instead, she seems to have sublimated everything into making money and knew how to play the market. When she died, she was worth about two hundred thousand."

"And she left all that to Daphne? Why?"

"Little Daphne seems to have been a shrewd cookie from an early age," Maltravers replied. "Always nice to great-aunt Constance. Sent birthday cards, buttered her up on both sides. The guy in Macclesfield says that Constance lapped it up."

" But why the marriage condition?" Tess asked.

"We can play psychiatrists over that if we want. Perhaps never having married was her great sorrow and she wanted to make sure Daphne didn't miss out on the experience."

"But she'd probably have married anyway without having to do so for money. Why should this Constance woman have tied it up like that?"

Maltravers shrugged. "Short of trying to make contact through a medium, I've only got guesses to offer. The fact is that she laid down the condition and it was absolute. Strange but true, children. Nowt as queer as folk, as they say in that part of the world."

"Why she did it doesn't matter, anyway, does it?" Tess observed. "The fact is that it's one hell of a motive for Daphne killing Caroline. How much will she actually get?"

"This is only a rough calculation by the solicitor, but prepare yourself." Maltravers could not resist a dramatic pause. "The original money was very intelligently invested in the boom of the early Eighties and they sold like crazy to beat the stock market crash in—when was it?—October 1987. We're talking well in excess of a million. Even with what Ted Owen's worth, that's got to be enough to kill for."

Tess gave a low whistle. "Ain't that the truth? But there's still a problem. I had lunch with Louella and she mentioned this. Will the police be able to prove anything?"

"That's occurred to me as well," he replied. "It's bloody suspicious, but a good defence lawyer could punch holes in it. Daphne Gillie had opportunity and a motive she kept shtoom about. But the bottom line is that it's only circumstantial."

"Well, you'll just have to give it to them and they can take it from there, I expect."

"Yes, but there was a message from Alan Bedford at that inquiry agency when I got back," Maltravers told her. "It's obviously got something to do with the Jenni Hilton business."

"But we've decided that's nothing to do with Caroline."

"I know, but I could offer him . . ." he hesitated. "Let's call it a trade off. I let him take this lot to the police and earn brownie points if he'll tell me about who's trying to find Jenni Hilton. If he wants to see me, perhaps he's having second thoughts about his client and protecting their confidentiality. It's worth a try."

"And what will you do if he does tell you?"

"That depends on who it is. It might actually be perfectly innocent and we can all sleep easy in our beds."

So she's ex-directory. Should have expected that, she's still trying to hide herself. Could have phoned to make sure she's there. Just have to go and chance it. If she's not in have to try again. The paper said she's got a son of her own now—nothing about a husband of course, probably a bastard—but he's somewhere miles away. Exeter is miles away, isn't it? He won't be there. There might be some man living with her, they're always talking about these women having toy-boys. Disgusting at her age, but they're all like bitches on heat. Can't get enough of it. Will he be there? If he is, have to go away and wait. Watch the house until he goes out. Don't go too early when he might still be around. Say first thing after dinner—Terry calls it lunch now. Bugger Terry, that's finished. Barry was worth ten of him. Barry . . . Barry . . . it's all right, love, Mum found the bayonet you left. Mum never forgot, Mum knew how much you loved her, she knew what that filth did to you. I'll find her grave afterwards and spit on it. Do you remember Mrs Tomkins at number twenty-seven? She always did that when she passed the cemetery where they buried her old man. She made us laugh, didn't she? Every time you came back, you asked her if she was still doing it. She thought you were wonderful. Always asking me about what you were doing, who you'd met now. Helped me a lot after . . . She's dead now as well. They put her with her old man. God, love, you'd have laughed at that wouldn't you? We were laughing all the time, weren't we? Nobody had a son like you, Barry. That's what they all used to tell me in Etruria Street. Maureen, you must be so proud of him they'd say. That big car, all those fancy friends and he still comes back to see you. They don't know how proud. I've got the bayonet. It's all right, love. You were listening when I swore on my knees that night, weren't You? You know Mum never let you down. Not long now. Tomorrow.

"Don't look round, but there's a woman at the corner table who's been trying not to stare at you ever since we walked in here. She's been awfully polite about it." Russell Hilton grinned at his mother. "That'll teach you to get your picture in the papers."

Jenni Hilton smiled ruefully and looked out of the window of the coffee shop towards the west front of Exeter Cathedral. As they had walked round it, she had noticed several people giving her second glances.

"Do you mind?" she asked. "You're not used to having a famous mother."

"Of course I don't mind. It's marvellous. Vanessa was incredibly impressed."

"Yes, but I don't want people referring to you as Jenni Hilton's son, as though that's all that was important about you. That's one of the problems when someone's famous. Their children feel as though they're living in a shadow."

"Well, I won't," he said firmly. "I'm going to be a doctor and that's all there is to it. You can go off and be as famous as you want again. You've brought me up and I hereby give you your freedom back."

She stuck her tongue out at him. "Don't be so damned patronising. My freedom isn't yours—or anybody else's—to hand out. I've been thinking about what I might do with it ever since you were old enough to leave the house on your own."

"Good. And what are you going to do with it? Start singing again? Go back on stage? Hey, will I be able to see you on TV with Terry Wogan?"

"No," she said firmly. "There are going to be very strict limits. Somebody called me with a film offer just before I left on Saturday, but—"

"A film offer?" he interrupted. "You never said. Something good?"

"Better than good but I'm not doing it."

"Why not?"

"Because . . . it's too long a story. I've been out of it all for too long. I can't plunge back in the deep end again. For God's sake, I'm . . ."

"You're making excuses." He looked across the table at her closely. "I always know when you start doing that. Why? What's the matter?"

"This is granting me my freedom is it? Third degree? Nothing's the matter. I just want to do it my way . . . sorry, that just slipped out. What was our rule about it?"

"Buy any recording of the bloody song and burn it as a penance." He reached across the table and took her hand. "Mum, if you want to be Jenni Hilton again then do it. I know how good you were. It'll be different now. No screaming kids and the Press chasing you every five minutes. Others have done it. I can handle it . . . There's nothing to handle from where I'm sitting. Don't worry about me."

"I don't. I worry about me."

Chapter Eighteen

I dreamt about Barry. We were living back in Etruria Street and he arrived. All my old neighbours were there and I was wearing that dress I wore when I went to the theatre. The car was shocking pink—just like the dress—and there were all sorts of people with him I didn't know. It was never like that, he always came on his own. There was a party and a cake with hundreds and hundreds of candles. It began to get silly like dreams always do. I was flying over Wapping and could see them all like ants, then it was just Barry and me watching West Ham play and Jack Forrest, who was our air-raid warden in the Blitz, was centre forward. Stupid that, he got his leg blown off when they bombed the docks. Then Barry started turning into Terry and . . . Oh, I don't know, it was all ridiculous. There was some bit when I was with our Miriam singing in the Dockers Arms and . . . No it's gone. But Barry was in the dream. Rita Wetherby used to say they were always near us. Swore her Tony came back and talked to her after he was killed in that road smash. He was a lovely lad. Bit like Barry, same sort of build. She died in that home at Tower Hamlets. She was a good age. And her big friend was . . . What time is it? Only six o'clock? Thought it must be later. Never get back to sleep now. Not today. Too much to think about. Barry was in the dream. Same as he always was. Didn't talk to me, but he was there. Just before I woke up. Rita Wetherby said that . . .

Alan Bedford held a blue plastic file between his hands and tapped it lightly on the desk before laying it down. From where he was sitting, Maltravers could see nothing written on the cover. Bedford sniffed slightly and leaned back in his chair.

"I am a little . . . concerned, Mr Maltravers."

"Really? Why?"

"Following our conversation I questioned my client and I'm not altogether happy with his answers."

"So your client is a man? You wouldn't even tell me that before."

Bedford gave a nod of appreciation. "Before we go any further, have you told me everything? Up to now, all I know is that someone called Barry Kershaw died in 1968, that he was a friend of Miss Hilton's and she was anxious his name did not appear in the article you wrote. You've not told me anything particularly suspicious."

"But someone's asked you to find her address," Maltravers added.

"And possibly for completely innocent reasons."

"Possibly," Maltravers echoed sceptically. "But after talking to me, you felt it necessary to ask whoever it is some questions and were so dissatisfied with what he said that you wanted to see me again. I think we should stop pussy-footing around here, Mr Bedford. Something's worrying you."

"Then you start," Bedford invited. "What haven't you told me?"

"I've told you everything I *know*. I haven't given you any theories so far because I can't prove anything."

"I think you're the sort of man whose theories would be interesting," Bedford remarked. "I'd like to hear them."

"I think that Jenni Hilton murdered Barry Kershaw."

"Now that *is* an interesting theory. What's your evidence?"

Bedford's face remained still as sculpture as Maltravers recounted the story of his visit to Jack Buxton in Porlock, what he had been told there and what he had been forced to conclude from it.

"But you have absolutely no evidence," Bedford commented at the end.

"Nothing at all," Maltravers admitted. "But yesterday I checked out another theory about something else and proved I was right. Perhaps I'm working well at the moment. Anyway, are you about to argue that what I'm suggesting is impossible?"

"No," Bedford conceded. "Although there could be other explanations. For instance—"

"Fuck other explanations!" Maltravers did not shout, but his voice had gone very hard. "Stop pissing me about, Mr Bedford. If I wanted to, I could dream up a dozen other explanations, but they won't necessarily knock the first one down. If I'm right, then whoever's asked you to find Jenni Hilton could be very dangerous. If anything happens to her, I will tell the police everything that's gone on, including the fact that you refused to co-operate. I don't know if you need a licence in this sort of business, but you've been bloody anxious to let me know how important your reputation is. Do you want to put that on the line?"

"Neither I nor this agency have done anything we know to have been illegal," Bedford replied levelly. "If you want to ask me to trace anybody's address here and now we'll do it."

"Even if I want to find them so I can kill them?" Maltravers snapped.

"I can't be held responsible for you not telling me your reasons," Bedford replied. "And it's certainly not the sort of thing that would occur to me."

Maltravers lit a cigarette. "All right, let's do this calmly. You know something that's made you want to talk to me again and I appreciate you're in a slightly tricky situation. Let me tell you something—and there are no preconditions on this—which could be useful to you and then perhaps you'll see your way to help me. A moment ago, I mentioned another theory I'd had. It's something the police have to be told about and I'm prepared to let you do that. It could certainly help your reputation with them. The fact is I'm convinced there's been another murder, tied up in a roundabout way with Jenni Hilton but really quite separate."

Bedford's face showed a flicker of interest. "No promises, but try me."

Maltravers was vaguely surprised that Bedford took no notes as he listened, then worked out that everything was probably being recorded anyway. He left a couple of silences as he spoke, ears straining for the hum of a recorder and thought he heard something from Bedford's side of the desk. It was academic; he was not bothered about it all being on tape. He sat back and waited for the reaction.

"You should open up in this business," Bedford said admiringly. "This agency would use you for a start."

"Praise from professionals is always welcome . . . Now do I get anything in return?"

Bedford revolved his chair and looked out of the window for a few moments. Suddenly he stood up. "Would you excuse me for just a couple of minutes? There's something I have to speak to my receptionist about."

"Of course." Maltravers did not turn round as he heard the door close behind him. The file Bedford had been holding when he arrived remained in the centre of the desk, next to the intercom on which he could have called the receptionist.

"Oh, the games people play," he muttered, then carefully played his own part, opening the file without disturbing its position. There was a single piece of paper inside and he memorised what was written on it instantly. When Bedford returned, Maltravers was back in his chair.

"Quite simply, Mr Maltravers, I would greatly like to help you, but you'll appreciate the problem," he said. "I am very grateful for the information you've given me about Caroline Owen's death and I'll have a word with the right people about it. Now I rather imagine you want to get off."

"Yes." Maltravers stood up and held out his hand. "If I ever meet anyone who needs a private inquiry agency, I'll recommend this one. I'll . . . assure them that the boss isn't a blabbermouth."

"Can't afford to be in this business. Goodbye."

Maltravers ignored the lift and took the stairs three at a time, dashing out into the City Road and running between slightly disapproving pedestrians until he reached *The Chronicle*'s offices. He chafed with impatience at getting through the security system, then pounded up to the first floor and burst into the features department. Mike Fraser looked up in surprise as he entered; unseemly haste in newspaper offices is restricted to minutes before deadline, not just before lunch.

"What the hell's the matter with you?" he demanded.

"I want to use a phone. Privately if possible."

"My office." Fraser indicated the second of a row of doors down one side of the room, then followed Maltravers through it. "Press five for an outside line."

"Thanks." Maltravers was muttering a number over and over to himself as he snatched up the phone. "Insignia Motors? Can I speak to Mr Kershaw, please? Pardon? When will he be back? About two o'clock? All right, I'll call him later."

He rang off and turned to Fraser. "Got a piece of paper? There's never any about in new technology offices."

"Here." Fraser crossed the room and took a memo pad from beneath a copy of that morning's edition. "Now what's going on?"

"Just let me write this down so I don't forget it." Maltravers scribbled Terry Kershaw's details from Bedford's file. "OK. One more call first though. I've left Jenni Hilton's number at home. Do you still have it?"

"Move over." Fraser sat down and logged on to the computer keyboard. He called up a file named "Contacts", then put "sf Jenni" in the command field. The screen went blank for a few seconds as the machine searched then text flicked back again, the cursor blinking at the end of the name. "There you are." He pushed back his chair as Maltravers leant forward to read, picking up the phone again to call the number. After holding for a half a minute, he rang off.

"No reply. She can't be back from Exeter yet."

"So if you haven't any more panic calls to make, you've got time to explain haven't you?"

Maltravers leant against the desk as the unaccustomed effort of running caught up with him. "I know who's looking for Jenni Hilton." By the time he had finished, he had calmed down, but the situation still frightened him.

"Let's take it a step at a time," Fraser said. "Has this Bedford found her and passed the address on?"

"I think he must have done—and that must have happened before I first went to see him on Monday. He's obviously got doubts about what's going on because he wanted to know more from me. If he hadn't already given Kershaw the address, he could have handled it himself and refused to if necessary."

"All right, so assume that Kershaw knew her address by

Monday. Nothing's happened since because she's away, but due back today. When?"

"I don't know. If she went by train, she'll arrive at Paddington, but I can't hang around waiting for every arrival."

"You could," Fraser corrected. "But you might miss her. Why not do a stakeout at her house? On the other hand, you still don't know why Kershaw wants to find her. There could be nothing to worry about."

"We've been through that. It's too devious to be trusted."

Fraser indicated the telephone. "Where did they say he was?"

"Just out. I didn't think to ask where."

"Let me try." Fraser took the memo pad from Maltravers and called Insignia Motors. "Mr Kershaw, please. Not there? Is there any way of reaching him? It's *The Chronicle* newspaper here and it's rather urgent . . . I see. Thank you. I'll call back then." He rang off. "Board meeting of some benevolent society. Can't be contacted. Sounds genuine."

"I'll control my panic for the time being," Maltravers said. "She's still not home anyway. I'm meeting Tess for lunch and I'll try after that. Incidentally, is Matt Hoffman in?"

"Look in home news. I saw him there earlier."

"Thanks. Look, Mike, I'm sorry to come in here like a bat out of hell, but—"

"Don't apologise," Fraser interrupted. "If you're right—and I can't knock down your suggestions—then we're mixed up here as well. I don't think the editor would be over the moon at having helped someone to commit murder, however inadvertently."

"Murder?" Maltravers winced. "It's not just me being hysterical, then. You think that as well."

"I think it's safest to think that. Perhaps we're both wrong. Anyway, I've got work to do. Go and see Matt."

Hoffman was leaving for lunch, but stopped and listened to Maltravers with increasing appreciation as he told him the story behind Caroline Owen's death.

"It could be *sub judice* in a hurry," he said. "But there's still the background stuff after the trial. Remember our deal. Nobody else gets it."

"Exclusive to *The Chronicle*," Maltravers promised. "Eat your heart out, Rupert Murdoch."

"See you around."

Not many people on the Tube. Wish that man would stop staring at me though. All wrong that. People never look at each other. They read the adverts, look at the floor, even out of the window in a tunnel. That's better, he's looking at that girl now. Don't want anyone to remember me. Who remembers? Close your eyes. Can you remember anyone else in the carriage—apart from him opposite? Of course you can't. They won't remember you, either. Where are we? Finchley Road? That's not on the Circle Line. God, it's the wrong train. Get off, Maureen. Damn, the doors are closing. What's the next stop? Can't see . . . it can't be Wembley Park, that's miles away. You stupid cow. You got on the Metropolitan line at King's Cross. It'll take ages to get back . . . Don't make a fuss. People will remember that. It's all right, there's plenty of time. That's a joke. After more than twenty years, what's another half-hour or so? What's an hour? It's all right, Barry. Mum made one of her mistakes, that's all. She'll put it right. Not long now. Back to . . . where is it? Baker Street. That's right. Then make sure you read the signs. Circle Line round to Sloane Square. Barry used to shop there. Bet it's not as good as it was then. Wait for me there, love. Mum's coming.

Reading was the last stop before London and Jenni Hilton picked up the memories which had started when they passed through on the way to Exeter. She'd been singing with the band in . . . the nightclub's name still wouldn't come back, but she could remember its tawdry glitter, the dirt and squalor of the dressing-room with its stench of stale beer behind the cheap sophistication of midnight blue wallpaper, vulgar lighting and plastic fittings of the main room. They'd been introduced as "one of London's top groups" and the set had been mainly standard rock numbers with only 'Smoke Gets in Your Eyes' to slow the tempo down and give the dancers the chance to smooch. While they were packing up afterwards, the compère had said there was a man asking for her and she had nearly refused to see him; letting herself be pulled after every gig had lost its teenage excitement. But she had agreed and it had been Stephen Delaney from Decca, who invited them to record a demo disc. That was when daydream talk of making it had turned into a roller coaster on which you screamed with delight and terror. She never slept with Stephen—Geoff the drummer did that—but he had persuaded her to go solo and held her hand through a lot of bad nights. It was through him that she had met Barry Kershaw.

As the train pulled out, she opened *The Face* again, burying the past before it became too agonising and hateful.

Tess glanced at her watch as Maltravers hurried down the stairs into Joe Allen's. "I thought you'd got lost. I've just ordered salads for both of us and asked them to hold yours."

"I want to eat fast," he told her. "I'll feel happier when I'm waiting for Jenni Hilton on her doorstep."

"What on earth for?"

"I now know who's been trying to find her address—and I think Bedford may have given it to him. He's called Terry Kershaw."

"Terry *Kershaw*? Is he a relation?"

"What else can he be?" Maltravers waved over a waiter and asked for his meal to be served with Tess's. "He works for a motor dealers on the North Circular near Hanger Lane. My guess is he's fairly high powered. He could be Barry Kershaw's son, although Louella never said anything about him having a family. Anyway, whoever he is, he's trouble. Jenni's due back today and I want to warn her. I've tried calling, but there's no reply."

"But what are you going to tell her?" Tess asked.

"The fact that someone called Kershaw's trying to find her should be enough. What she's prepared to tell me is something else. Oh, good."

He leant back as the waiter arrived with their food, said he didn't want to test the house white and told Tess the details of his visit to Bedford as they began to eat. When they finished, he asked for the bill then went to phone Jenni Hilton again. He was about to ring off when she answered.

"Jenni Hilton? Gus Maltravers. You're back."

"I've only been in a few minutes. I was upstairs when the phone rang. How are you? I loved your piece and thank you for keeping out—"

"I'm not calling for compliments," he interrupted. "There's something important I've got to tell you. I can come round and explain in detail, but the point is that . . ."

"Pardon? This is a dreadful line. Can you speak up? Did you say . . . Oh, hell, there's someone at the door. Hang on a second." She put down the receiver.

"Good-afternoon. I've come for the RSPCA envelope."

"Sorry? What envelope?"

"We put them through all the doors the other day. It's for the animals. You know, the charity."

"Yes, of course. I've been away. Look, I'm just on . . . No wait a moment. I'll get my bag."

She went into the front room and was searching for her purse when she heard the front door close. It didn't usually do that on its own. Pulling out a ten-pound note she turned round and saw the woman standing in the doorway.

"Oh. I didn't mean . . . It's all right. Here you are. You've got a tin or something? Oh, in your bag . . ."

In Joe Allen's, Maltravers stiffened as he heard a scream. "Hello! Hello! Jenni!" There was the sound as though something or someone had fallen and another cry, fainter than the first. "Jenni! What is it? Shit and derision!"

He slammed the phone down and almost ran back to the table where the waiter was just placing the bill by his chair.

"Thanks. Keep the change." Maltravers grabbed a random handful of notes from his wallet, dropped them on the plate and turned to a startled Tess. "Come on."

By the time she reached the top of the stairs, she saw him racing towards Burleigh Street. She sprinted after him and caught up as he reached the Strand.

"What the hell's the matter?" she demanded.

"Don't know, but I think it's serious." He waved violently at a taxi, but the driver didn't see him. "Damn. There's another . . . Christ Almighty!"

He was glaring in frustration as a second cab ignored him,

when a piercing whistle shrieked from behind and the driver glanced towards the sound and pulled into the kerb. As he turned round, Tess was lowering the fingers of her right hand from her mouth.

"Girl Guides," she explained. "Stopped doing it when I decided it wasn't ladylike. Tell me inside."

They dashed along the pavement and scrambled in. Maltravers stooped forward to speak to the driver through the sliding glass panel, taking out his wallet again. "Twelve Cheyne Street, Chelsea. And this is for breaking all records. We're in one hell of a hurry."

The driver glanced at the twenty-pound note appreciatively and the vehicle made a U-turn across the traffic as though the flashing indicator projected some magic beam which cleared roads instantly as Maltravers half fell back into the seat beside Tess.

"I take it that something is up," she said.

"In spades," Maltravers replied grimly, and told her what he had heard down the phone. "Christ knows what's happened. Come *on*!"

He groaned as the cab was momentarily stuck behind a bus before breaking free, speeding across Trafalgar Square, under Admiralty Arch and into The Mall. Passing in front of Buckingham Palace, they went through a gap between two cars which appeared narrower than the vehicle itself—a standard manœuvre among London cabbies—and headed towards Pimlico. The traffic lights seemed endless, but after what felt like an eternity they reached Cheyne Street and pulled up outside Jenni Hilton's house. Maltravers checked his watch.

"Under fifteen minutes at this time of day. We picked the right cab. Thanks a lot. Here you are."

"Breaks the monotony, this sort of fare." The driver winked at him as he accepted the money. "Someone having a baby, is it?"

"That sort of thing."

Tess was already at the front door holding the bell down. "What do we do if there's no reply?"

"Break a window if necessary. I'm not in the mood to . . ."

He grabbed hold of the brass knocker and hammered it fiercely against the door. "Jesus Christ, answer!"

A delay of seconds was too long for him. He leapt off the steps to where the cab was about to pull away. "Hang on. We need the police. Can you call them on your radio?"

The driver looked at him guardedly. "I got you here, friend. I don't want to get mixed up in anything else."

"There isn't time to explain, but this is a crisis! For Christ's sake, can you grasp that?"

As Maltravers glared desperately through the open window, it seemed for a moment as though the cabbie was going to drive off, but then he pushed the gear stick into neutral and reached down for something on the floor by his feet.

"This isn't happening. Right?" he said as he stepped out. He went up to the steps and inserted the crowbar he was carrying between door and frame next to the lock then leant his weight against it. Wood protested then split as the door sprang open.

"If you need the coppers, then you call them," he said. "I haven't got time to waste making statements. This is none of my business and you didn't see me break this door. OK?"

"Never saw you in my life," Maltravers agreed. "Thanks a lot."

The driver turned away as they entered the house. On the hall table, the receiver was still lying by the telephone. Maltravers took hold of Tess's arm and pulled her behind him.

"Careful," he warned. "I don't know what we're walking into." Keeping close to the wall, he cautiously moved to where he could see into the front room, one eye on the stairs rising out of the hall. Tess watched him, anxious and apprehensive. Maureen Kershaw appeared in the doorway, blood trickling from a cut on her forehead. Maltravers had never seen more hatred in a human face.

"Where is she?" The question hissed with insane urgency. "Where's the bitch who killed my Barry?" Her eyes darted to the right and glittered with madness as she saw Tess. It was as though Maltravers was invisible. "There you are. Nowhere to hide now, is there?"

Stunned by her appearance, Maltravers almost froze as she leapt down the hall. As she passed him and Tess screamed, he savagely kicked the old woman's leg then collapsed on her as she fell with a cry of pain. The bayonet flew out of her hand and Tess snatched it from the floor.

"Find Jenni!" Maltravers gasped as he pinned the struggling Maureen Kershaw down. "At least she hasn't killed her."

Chapter Nineteen

Tess ignored the front room; if Jenni Hilton had been there, Maureen Kershaw would not have come looking for her. The sitting-room was empty, as was the kitchen at the rear of the house, and the door leading to the walled garden was still bolted on the inside. She dashed back into the hall where Maltravers was helping the old woman to her feet and raced upstairs. As she burst through the first door she saw, there was a cry of terror. Jenni Hilton was standing in the far corner, staring at her in horror.

"It's all right . . . Christ, sorry." Tess threw down the bayonet she was still holding. "I'm Tess Davy. Gus's girlfriend. He rang you from Joe Allen's and heard . . . hold on!"

She dashed across the room as Jenni Hilton's eyes glazed and she began to crumple. She caught her below the shoulders. The left arm felt sticky and the woman cried out in pain. Tess instinctively pulled her hand away from the purple material of the dress and saw that her palm was blotched with red.

"Come on." She guided Jenni to the edge of the bed and sat her down, then took hold of the edges of the slash in the dress's sleeve and ripped it wider. The wound gaped like an open mouth but was not deep.

"My first aid's rusty, but it doesn't look serious," Tess said reassuringly. There was a box of tissues on the bedside table and she grabbed a handful, pressing them on to the running blood. "Got any bandages?"

"Bathroom," Jenni mumbled. "In the cupboard."

Tess settled her against the headboard of the bed. "Stay upright and hold those tissues in place. Back in a moment."

As she stepped on to the landing, Maltravers appeared at the top of the stairs.

"How are things down there?" she asked.

"She's passed out. Where's Jenni?"

Tess indicated the bedroom. "I'm getting something to patch her up. She's all right."

When Tess returned with lint, a roll of bandage, Dettol and sticking plaster, Maltravers was sitting next to Jenni Hilton, holding her hand. He supported her as Tess bound up the wound and made a makeshift sling from a scarf she found in a chest of drawers.

"That'll do for the time being," she said as she finished. "It doesn't look as though it needs stitches, but you ought to go to hospital."

"No." Jenni Hilton had said nothing while Tess had been treating her, but now her voice was firm and determined. "I just need a drink. Where's . . . where's that woman?"

"Downstairs," Maltravers told her. "You know who she is, of course."

"No, I don't. I've never seen her before in my life."

"Perhaps not, but you still know she's Barry Kershaw's mother."

Jenni Hilton sank back against the headboard and closed her eyes. "How much do you know?" she asked wearily.

"Not all of it, but a lot," he replied. "When I telephoned, I was trying to warn you that someone called Kershaw was looking for you. I'm sorry I couldn't let you know in time."

His head whirled towards the bedroom door as he heard a sound from the hall. "Hell, she's come round. Wait here."

As he reached the top of the stairs, Maureen Kershaw was standing outside the front-room door, supporting herself against a chair. She glared up at him resentfully as he went down.

"Who are you?" she demanded as he got to the last step. "The Old Bill?"

"No," he said. "If I was, you'd be in a lot of trouble. The police don't like things like this and neither do I."

"Then you can get knotted." The fierceness of her voice still retained the driving force of a rage which had sustained her for twenty years. "This is nobody's business but mine."

"And Terry's," Maltravers commented.

"Bugger Terry," she snapped contemptuously. "He's not worth spit. Barry was ten times the son to me, and that bitch killed him. Where is she? Hiding like a rat again?"

"She's upstairs," Maltravers told her. "And I think it might sort a few things out if we get the two of you together."

"I'll have her," Maureen Kershaw threatened. "With my bare hands I'll have her."

Maltravers drew a deep breath as mother love disfigured to animal fury snarled at him. Face filled with a counterbalancing menace, he stepped forward and Maureen Kershaw looked suddenly uncertain.

"Not while I'm here," he told her. "I have no wish to hit you again, but don't kid yourself that I won't. This bloody mess has got to be cleared up before it goes any further. Now get in here!"

For a moment, she resisted as he took hold of her arm, then her body went slack as he tightened his grip. He led her into the front room and sat her on the settee. One of the dining chairs was overturned and on the floor was a Dresden figure, its head broken off. He poured a brandy from the decanter on a corner table and handed it to her.

"Drink that and stay here."

She hesitated, then accepted the glass and held it in both hands. As she sipped from it, he went back into the hall, picked up the telephone receiver hanging from its wire, remade the connection and rang Insignia Motors.

"Mr Kershaw? My name's Augustus Maltravers. You don't know me, but I'm calling from number twelve Cheyne Street and I think you know that address. Your mother's here and I'd like you to come at once."

"What's happened?" Kershaw sounded horrified.

"Nothing too serious, fortunately. But there are some things that have got to be sorted out and they involve you."

"Is she all right?"

"As all right as she'll ever be. There's no point in wasting time talking on the phone. Just get over here."

"I'll be there as soon as I can. I . . . I'm sorry, but . . . No, you're right, we're wasting time. Are the police there?"

"No—and I'm hoping it might not be necessary to call them. I don't think it would do any good."

"I'm on my way."

Kershaw rang off and Maltravers went back into the front room where Maureen Kershaw was still on the settee. He poured another brandy, a whisky for Tess and a gin for himself and took them all upstairs. Jenni Hilton looked better than when he had left her, colour seeping back into a face that had looked like parchment when he had first seen her.

"Here you are." He handed out the glasses. "We all need these. Then I want you to come downstairs so we can talk."

"I'm going nowhere near that woman!" Jenni protested angrily. "I just want her out of this house."

"So she can come back?" Maltravers demanded. "Do you have any idea how much she hates you? She's been hating you for more than twenty years because she's convinced that you killed her son."

Jenni Hilton stared at him. "She's mad."

"And dangerous," he added. "And by saying she's mad, are you also saying that she's wrong?" There was a long silence. "Well, are you?"

"Why did you have to start prying into this?" Jenni asked bitterly. "It was all a very long time ago. Does it really matter to you? Really?"

"Frankly, no," he replied. "It was none of my business, and if I hadn't wanted to find out more about Caroline Owen's death, I'd probably have forgotten about Barry Kershaw. But that woman downstairs wouldn't have done."

"And what good will it be talking to a madwoman?"

"I'm not sure, but I've just rung Terry Kershaw and he's on his way here. At the moment, it seems a better alternative than calling the police. They could rake up a lot of things which are better left alone."

"He's right," Tess said. "Louella Sinclair told us that everyone was convinced that Barry Kershaw was murdered, but that was years ago and doesn't concern us. It might not even be true. But if the police are brought in, a lot of people could be in trouble. Including you."

Jenni gave Maltravers a strange smile. "Why should that

worry you? Don't you like the idea of your teenage goddess being destroyed?"

"I stopped worshipping a long time ago," he said. "It's just that by chance I'm in a position to make decisions that policemen might not like but I think are for the best. Punishing Maureen Kershaw won't help anyone and neither will reopening the file on her son's death. Perhaps it can be avoided."

"Journalists aren't usually so altruistic. They prefer splashing people's private lives all over their newspapers to helping them."

He shrugged. "I told you I wasn't like that when we first met. Maybe this will finally convince you. Anyway, downstairs."

Tess supported Jenni Hilton as they went back to the front room. Maureen Kershaw had not moved, but her eyes flashed as she saw Jenni Hilton again.

"Just behave yourself," Maltravers warned her. "Terry's on his way."

"Terry? What bloody good is he going to be? You should have left him out of it."

"He's already in whether you like it or not. He shouldn't be long. While we're waiting, what happened here? As far as I can make out, you got in one slash with that bayonet, then it looks as though Jenni threw that piece of Dresden and knocked you out."

"Right little Sherlock Holmes, aren't you?" Maureen Kershaw said sarcastically. "Who are you two, anyway? Friends of hers?"

"Not in the way you mean it, but it'll take too long to explain. I know a certain amount about Barry, and—"

"Who from?" the old woman interrupted sharply.

"People who knew him back in the Sixties."

"Filth." Maureen Kershaw looked at Jenni Hilton. "Like her. All smooth and toffee-nosed, pretending they liked him when they needed his help then lying through their teeth when he was dead. You know nothing about him, mister. I'm his mother. I do."

"Did he ever take drugs?"

She sneered. "You see? They've been lying to you as well. That's what they said at the inquest and everyone believed them. They weren't fit to clean his shoes and neither are you."

"But he'd been taking drugs the night he died. The police said that."

"That's what they said. Money can buy anything you want. But don't expect me to believe it, because it wasn't true. Got it?"

A car drew up outside and a moment later they heard someone step through the broken door and a man appeared in the front-room doorway. Thin, drawn face beneath short black hair was tense with anxiety. He ignored everyone except Maureen Kershaw.

"Mum! Are you all right?"

As he moved towards her, she gestured him away. "No thanks to you. I told you to forget all about this. This is just me and Barry."

Terry Kershaw stopped uncertainly in the centre of the room as she stared at him in revulsion, then shook his head helplessly.

"I think you need a drink as well, Mr Kershaw." Maltravers stood up. "Incidentally, I don't think you've met Jenni Hilton."

Kershaw turned away from his mother. For a few moments he and Jenni looked at each other without speaking, then he indicated the sling.

"Did she do that? I'm sorry."

"So you should be," said Maltravers. "You're the one who led her here. What do you want?"

"Whisky. On its own." Kershaw did not take his eyes off Jenni Hilton as he replied. "I shouldn't have done that, but . . . I can't explain it. It started so long ago and I couldn't refuse. I don't think anyone who hadn't been through it could understand."

Jenni Hilton lowered her head. "It doesn't matter," she said softly.

"Here you are." Maltravers gave Kershaw his whisky. "Now you three are going to listen to me because you can't talk to each other. You're all on the edge of very serious trouble if any of this comes out, but it might be avoided if everybody uses some sense."

He went back to his chair and sat down. "In 1968 your brother—and your son—died. That's the one fact that we know and the one fact that nothing can be done about. He may have been murdered, but nobody has any evidence to prove it and it's not likely to appear after all this time. You, Mrs Kershaw, wanted revenge and convinced yourself that this lady killed him. I rather suspect you have tried to convince Terry of that as well. But you don't know if you're right. Today you've attacked her and might have killed her if we hadn't arrived. What were you going to do after that? Do you really imagine you'd have got away with it? I'd have made bloody sure you didn't for a start."

"I didn't know anything about you."

"Well, you do now. And I know you. I also know that Terry found this address for you. It's the end of the road, Mrs Kershaw, unless you want to risk going to jail . . . and what would Barry have thought about his mother behind bars? If he loved you as much as you obviously loved him, he'd never have wanted that. But that's what's going to happen if you try anything like this again. I mean it."

Maltravers kept his face very stern as Maureen Kershaw began to weep angry tears. "You don't know how much I loved him. He was all that mattered and they took him away from me."

"And nothing's going to bring him back. All you've got are memories, but I'm sure they're good ones."

She stared into her glass as Terry Kershaw looked at her pleadingly. "Listen to him, Mum. You've still got me."

Maltravers half rose from his chair as Maureen Kershaw sobbed violently and threw her glass on the carpet as she stood up.

"I don't want *you*! Why wasn't it you who died?"

Terry Kershaw stared blankly at his mother before she walked out of the room. Then he stood up and shouted after her desperately.

"Mum!"

There was no response as they heard her leave the house. He was about to follow her when Maltravers stopped him.

"She'll manage," he said. "She found her way here, she'll find her way home. She's certainly not going to talk to you at the moment."

Kershaw gazed at him, anguished and bewildered. "She's my mother."

"No. She's Barry's mother." Kershaw stared at him uncomprehendingly, then accepted everything he meant.

"Yes, she is," he said sadly. "I expect I've always known that." He turned to Jenni Hilton. "I can imagine what you think of me, but I never wanted to hurt you, however it looks. I won't insult you by trying to apologise again. I'm just grateful that it was nothing worse. Goodbye."

Maltravers went with him to the front door. Kershaw looked up and down Cheyne Street, but there was no sign of anyone.

"I don't think she'll come here again," Maltravers assured him.

"No," he agreed. "You hit her hard in there. I should have done that a long time ago."

"It must be almost impossible when it's your mother."

"Not almost. Totally. I've spent a fortune on counselling over this and I still couldn't break free." Kershaw glanced at him. "Are you really not going to tell the police?"

"You heard what I said. There's no need and there's no point. Your mother's just going to have to live with a few things."

"So am I." Terry Kershaw turned abruptly, got into his car and drove away.

Tess was pouring more drinks as Maltravers returned to the front room.

"That woman is very bad news," she said feelingly. "Are you sure she took in what you told her?"

"I think the message got home. Ending up in jail was never part of her plan of revenge and it should eventually sink in that that's what will happen if she tries anything again." He smiled at Jenni Hilton. "Try not to worry about it."

"I won't. She'll hardly chase me to California."

"Is that what you're going to do?"

"It's what I should have done in the first place. There's work there if I want it and I'll feel safer than in London."

"At least think it over," he said. "This isn't a good time to make decisions. What will Russell think?"

"He told me while I was in Exeter that he was giving me my freedom back. I'll take him up on it."

"Pity. It would have been good to see you perform here

again." Maltravers picked up his glass. "How's the arm? You really should go to hospital with it, but they might start asking difficult questions."

"Tess said it wasn't too bad and I think it's nearly stopped bleeding. I'll go and see my private doctor. There shouldn't be any problems."

"That reminds me," said Maltravers. "There's a bayonet around here somewhere which ought to be got rid of. Where is it?"

"On the floor upstairs," Tess told him. "I terrified Jenni by carrying it into the bedroom when I was looking for her."

"We'll take it with us," Maltravers said. "Perhaps I'll drop it in the Thames one night. That'll be a suitably dramatic gesture."

Jenni Hilton accepted her refilled glass from Tess. "I forgot to say thank you somewhere. I went to pieces when she attacked me and was like a gibbering idiot in that bedroom. I didn't even have the sense to run out of the house or climb through the window. All I could think about was that the telephone was downstairs and I'd never got around to having an upstairs extension installed. Stupid."

"Not the sort of time when people necessarily think straight." Maltravers paused for a moment. "Look, you don't have to answer this and if you do it goes no further than us three. It's just that I'd like to know if—"

"If I murdered Barry?" she finished as he hesitated uncertainly. "You said that his death was none of your business."

He shrugged. "Fair enough. Sorry, forget it."

"I'd like to be able to do that." She swallowed half her drink, then stared at the fireplace as she continued. "All right. You probably just saved my life and deserve some answers. I think I can trust you enough to keep it to yourself. Before the party, I told Barry I'd go to bed with him and put on one hell of an act that I was looking forward to it. After everyone left, he was half drunk and got excited when I said I had something we could take that would make it even better. All he could talk about as he took the LSD was what he was going to do to me and it nearly made me sick just listening to him. He was laughing and crying and mauling me. I told him I wanted to look at the moon and opened the french doors on to the balcony. We stood there and I said wouldn't it be wonderful to be able to fly . . . and he said that he could."

She finished the drink. "He was giggling when he jumped, but then he went quiet. I didn't look down until I heard him hit the ground. Before I went home, the phone rang and it was some journalist. I shouldn't have answered it, but it made no difference. For some reason, I was one of the first people the police came to see and they mentioned they'd found the LSD in his body. I told them I'd suspected he took drugs. It was a lie of course, but they believed it, perhaps they wanted to. They were as responsible as anyone for the story getting around. Anyway, other people backed it up and even said so at the inquest. We never plotted it, it just happened."

She gestured towards where Maureen Kershaw had been sitting. "Of course I'd seen her before. At the inquest. But she was younger then and I didn't recognise her today. She's changed."

She looked up at Maltravers. "So now you know. I've never told anyone before."

"And you haven't now," he said quietly.

"Don't you want to know why I did it?"

"I think I already do. I went to Porlock and talked to Jack Buxton at the weekend. I also understand why you ran away."

"Oh, Gus Maltravers." Sarcastic appreciation filled her voice. "What a clever journalist you are."

"And not the sort you're used to," he reminded her. "Just one other thing—and this is certainly not my business but it crossed my mind—is Jack Russell's father? I don't think he can be."

"Oh, no. I met Desmond in New York about a year after I quit. I was very fond of him—we still keep in touch—but I didn't want to marry him. Russell was our nice accident. He's the most important thing in my life." Tears suddenly glistened at the corners of her eyes. "Like Barry was for his mother. Dear God, which of us is the more guilty?"

"That's another thing which isn't my business," Maltravers said.

*

Daphne Gillie was charged with the murder of Caroline Owen, but was released on bail through the skill of her lawyer. In the interval before the trial, she and Ted Owen married. Matt Hoffman managed to arrange a place for Maltravers on the Old Bailey Press bench for what had become a major media event as she faced a charge of murder with her now husband as an accessory. After the prosecution had finished, one of London's leading QCs asked the judge that the jury be sent out of the court then ripped the case to pieces in their absence. The police had not found a single witness who had seen Daphne anywhere near Tottenham Court Road Tube station, let alone on the platform, on the night Caroline had died. Mr Owen was a wealthy man, earning in excess of a quarter of a million pounds a year; his wife's salary was a hundred thousand pounds. Neither of the accused had ever lied to the police and could only be criticised for keeping quiet about Daphne's legacy; this was regrettable, but they had been understandably concerned that the police would jump to the wrong conclusion—which had now happened. Both his clients were highly respectable people and, if required, the defence would call witnesses who would vouch for their probity. There was not one scrap of evidence, nothing more than supposition which did not amount to . . . As elegant, persuasive phrases filled the courtroom, Maltravers grudgingly admired the barrister's performance and could see exactly where it was leading. The jury were recalled and the judge instructed them to return verdicts of not guilty.

Outside, Maltravers and Hoffman watched a posse of photographers shouting excitedly at Ted and Daphne Owen as they stood smiling with their arms around each other, facing a constant broadside of dazzling flashlights. They repeatedly kissed when they were asked to as a group of their friends cheered and shouted congratulations. One waved a bottle of champagne, a bow of silver ribbon tied round the neck.

"Bang goes the real story," Hoffman commented sourly. "The police are bloody sure they did it and so am I. What a pisser. How do you feel about it?"

"Fairly sick, but I'll take it philosophically." Maltravers pulled on his coat as rain began to spit. "They're not the first to get away with murder. Come on, I need a drink. I'll tell you another story you can't use either. What is it that journalists say about news stories? The best ones never get into print."